"Why do you think I'm worth saving?"

"Because you're a good guy. You've spent your life being a hero for your country. You're smart, occasionally funny and breathtakingly handsome, though I wouldn't let that go to your head. Good looks rarely make up for a lousy disposition."

A smile tugged at his lips. "I'll try to remember that."

Kelly regarded him seriously. "Michael, there are a lot of blessings in your life. You should try counting them, instead of focusing on what you've lost."

"I will," he promised, his own expression suddenly serious. "I hope you won't mind if I put you at the top of the list."

Kelly's breath caught in her throat. "Dammit, why did you have to say something so sweet?" she asked. "I was just getting comfortable being furious with you."

He reached over and gently brushed away a tear streaking down her face. "Well, now, I couldn't have that, could I?"

Dear Reader,

Our resolution is to start the year with a bang in Silhouette Special Edition! And so we are featuring Peggy Webb's *The Accidental Princess*—our pick for this month's READERS' RING title. You'll want to use the riches in this romance to facilitate discussions with your friends and family! In this lively tale, a plain Jane agrees to be the local Dairy Princess and wins the heart of the bad-boy reporter who wants her story…among other things.

Next up, Sherryl Woods thrills her readers once again with the newest installment of THE DEVANEYS—*Michael's Discovery.* Follow this ex-navy SEAL hero as he struggles to heal from battle—and save himself from falling hard for his beautiful physical therapist! Pamela Toth's *Man Behind the Badge,* the third book in her popular WINCHESTER BRIDES miniseries, brings us another stunning hero in the form of a flirtatious sheriff, whose wild ways are numbered when he meets—and wants to rescue—a sweet, yet reclusive woman with a secret past. Talking about secrets, a doctor hero is stunned when he finds a baby—maybe even *his* baby—on the doorstep in Victoria Pade's *Maybe My Baby,* the second book in her BABY TIMES THREE miniseries. Add a feisty heroine to the mix, and you have an instant family.

Teresa Southwick delivers an unforgettable story in *Midnight, Moonlight & Miracles.* In it, a nurse feels a strong attraction to her handsome patient, yet she doesn't want him to discover the *real* connection between them. And Patricia Kay's *Annie and the Confirmed Bachelor* explores the blossoming love between a self-made millionaire and a woman who can't remember her past. Can their romance survive?

This month's lineup is packed with intrigue, passion, complex heroines and heroes who never give up. Keep your own resolution to live life romantically, with a treat from Silhouette Special Edition. Happy New Year, and happy reading!

Karen Taylor Richman
Senior Editor

Please address questions and book requests to:
Silhouette Reader Service
U.S.: 3010 Walden Ave., P.O. Box 1325, Buffalo, NY 14269
Canadian: P.O. Box 609, Fort Erie, Ont. L2A 5X3

SHERRYL WOODS

MICHAEL'S DISCOVERY

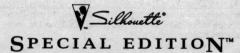

SPECIAL EDITION™

Published by Silhouette Books

America's Publisher of Contemporary Romance

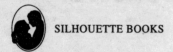

SILHOUETTE BOOKS

ISBN 0-373-24513-0

MICHAEL'S DISCOVERY

Visit Silhouette at www.eHarlequin.com

Printed in U.S.A.

Books by Sherryl Woods

Silhouette Special Edition

Silhouette Desire

Silhouette Books

SHERRYL WOODS

has written more than seventy-five novels. She also operates her own bookstore, Potomac Sunrise, in Colonial Beach, Virginia. If you can't visit Sherryl at her store, then be sure to drop her a note at P.O. Box 490326, Key Biscayne, FL 33149 or check out her Web site at www.sherrylwoods.com.

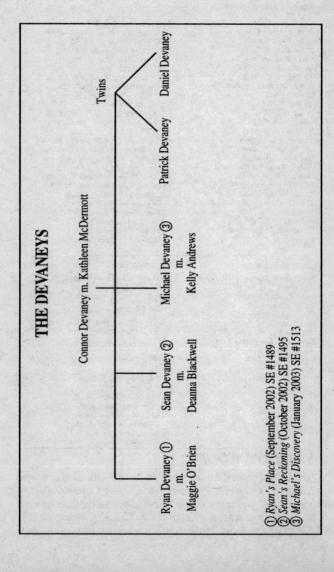

THE DEVANEYS

Connor Devaney m. Kathleen McDermott

Ryan Devaney ①
m.
Maggie O'Brien

Sean Devaney ②
m.
Deanna Blackwell

Michael Devaney ③
m.
Kelly Andrews

Twins

Patrick Devaney

Daniel Devaney

① *Ryan's Place* (September 2002) SE #1489
② *Sean's Reckoning* (October 2002) SE #1495
③ *Michael's Discovery* (January 2003) SE #1513

Prologue

Even through the haze of pain, Michael was aware of the charged atmosphere in his San Diego hospital room. The doctors had just delivered their dire predictions for his future with the Navy SEALs. Nurse Judy, normally a fountain of inconsequential, cheery small talk, was fluffing his pillow with total concentration, carefully avoiding his gaze. Clearly everyone was waiting for his explosion of outrage, his cries of despair. Michael refused to give them the satisfaction—not just yet anyway.

"Okay," he said, gritting his teeth against the hot, burning pain radiating through his leg. "That's the worst-case scenario. What's the best I can hope for?"

His doctors—the best orthopedic doctors anywhere, according to his boss—exchanged the kind of look that Michael recognized. He'd seen it most often when an entire op was about to go up in flames. He'd been seeing it a lot since a sniper had blasted one bullet through his knee, then shattered his thigh bone with another. The head injury that had left him in a coma had been minor by comparison. The patchwork repairs to his bones had apparently just begun.

He still wasn't sure how long he'd been out of touch, left for dead by the terrorist cell he'd penetrated. He did know that had it not been for a desperate, last-ditch effort by his team members, he would have died in that hellhole. He should be grateful to be alive, but if his career was over, how could he be? Though he was determined not to show it, despair was already clawing at him.

"Just tell me, dammit!" he commanded the expressionless doctors.

"That *was* the best-case scenario," the older of the two men told him. "Worst case? You could still lose your leg."

Michael felt a roar of protest building in his chest, but years of containing his emotions kept him silent. Only a muscle working in his jaw gave away the anguish he was feeling.

His entire identity was tied up with being a Navy SEAL. The danger, the adrenaline rush, the skill, the teamwork—all of it gave him a sense of purpose. With it, he was a hero. Without it, he was just an ordinary guy.

And years ago, abandoned by his parents, separated from his brothers, Michael had made a vow that he would never settle for being ordinary. Ordinary kids got left behind. Ordinary men were a dime a dozen. He'd driven himself to excel from his first day of kindergarten right on through SEAL training. Now these doctors were telling him he'd never excel again, at least not physically. He might not even walk…at least not for a long, long time. As for losing his leg, that was not an option.

With that in mind, he leveled a look first at one man, then the other. "Let's see to it that doesn't happen, okay? I'm a mean son of a gun when I'm pissed, and that would really piss me off."

Nurse Judy chuckled, then bit off the reaction. "Sorry."

Michael shifted slightly, winced at the pain, then winked at her. "It always pays to keep a man who's itchy to use a knife aware of the consequences."

She touched a cool hand to his cheek and studied him with concern. Since she was at least fifty, he had a hunch the gesture was nothing more than a subtle check of his temperature. The woman hadn't kept her hands to herself since he'd been brought in two days ago with a raging fever from the infection that had spread from his leg wounds throughout his body. She'd been with him when he was rushed straight into surgery to try to repair the damage that had occurred halfway across the world. The doctors in the field hospital had done their best, but there had been little doubt that his injuries would require a higher level of medical skill.

He gave the nurse a pale imitation of his usually devastating smile. She was beginning to show signs of exhaustion, but she hadn't left his side, unless she'd stolen a catnap while he'd been out of it in the operating room. Obviously she'd been hired by his bosses because she took her private-duty nursing assignments seriously. And given his own level of security clearance, hers was probably just as high in case he started muttering classified information in his sleep.

"How about some pain meds?" she asked. "You've been turning me down all morning. This stoic act of yours is beginning to get old. You'll heal faster in the long run if you're not in agony."

"I wanted to be alert for the prognosis," he reminded her.

"And now?"

"I think I'd better stay alert to make sure those two stay the hell away from my leg."

Just then there was a flurry of activity at the doorway, a hushed conversation, and then two tall, dark-haired men were pushing their way inside, ignoring the doctors' protests that no visitors were allowed.

"Why not take that medication, bro? We're here now. Nothing's going to happen to your leg on our watch," the older of the two said, pulling a chair up beside the bed and shooting a warning look at the doctors that would have intimidated an entire fleet of the Navy's finest.

An image floated through Michael's hazy memory. He looked again and suddenly a name came to him, a name he hadn't thought of in years. "Ryan?"

"It's me, kid," his oldest brother responded, squeezing Michael's hand. "Sean's here, too."

To his total chagrin, Michael blinked back tears. So many years, but there had been a time when he'd shadowed his two older brothers everywhere they went. They had been his heroes, at least until they had deserted him. To a shaken four-year-old that's how it had seemed on the day he'd been taken away to live with a different foster family—as if the cornerstones of his world had abandoned him. Coming on the heels of his parents' vanishing with the twins, it had been too much. He'd pushed all thoughts of the other Devaneys from his mind, kept them locked away in a dark place where the memories couldn't hurt him.

And now, all these years later, his older brothers at least were back, the timely arrival just as mysterious as the untimely disappearance.

"How did you find me?" he asked, his voice thick with emotion. "Where did you come from?"

"We'll get into all that later. Right now, you need some sleep," Ryan soothed.

Michael studied him, then sought out Sean. He would have recognized them anywhere, he thought. It was like looking in the mirror: the same black hair—even if his was military crewcut short—the same blue eyes. They'd all inherited Connor Devaney's roguish good looks, for better or for worse.

Their father had been a handsome devil, one generation removed from Ireland and with a gift for blarney. An image of him crept into Michael's head from time to time, always accompanied by deeply entrenched bitterness. If there was a God in heaven, Connor Devaney would rot in hell for taking his wife and their youngest sons and walking away from Michael, Sean and Ryan.

"Lieutenant, how about that pain medication now?" Nurse Judy asked gently.

Michael wanted to protest. He had so many questions he wanted to ask his brothers. But one glance at the way Ryan and Sean had settled in reassured him that they weren't going anywhere. Nor was any surgeon going to get anywhere near his damaged leg as long as *they* were around.

"Sure," he said, finally giving in.

Michael felt the prick of a needle in his arm, the slow retreat of pain and then his eyes drifted shut and for the first time since he'd been flown home to California, he felt safe enough to fall into a deep, untroubled sleep.

Chapter One

Six months later, Boston

Michael maneuvered his wheelchair across the floor and set the lock. He eyed the sofa and debated whether its comfort was worth the effort it would take to heave himself out of the chair. Every damn day was filled with such inconsequential challenges. After years of trying to sort through the life-and-death logistics of SEAL missions, it grated on him that the simple decision of where to sit to watch another boring afternoon of television took on such importance.

"You want some help?" Ryan asked, his expression neutral.

Over the past few weeks, when his brother had been popping in and out of California on a regular basis, Michael had learned to recognize that look. It meant that Ryan was feeling sorry for him and was trying not to show it.

The attempt was pretty lame, but Ryan was actually better at it than Sean. Sean's obvious pity was almost more than Michael could take, which was one reason Ryan had been designated to pick him up at the airport and to help him settle into his new apartment.

Michael had discovered that the grown-up Ryan was a low-key kind of guy. He ran his own Irish pub and had settled into family life with a woman named Maggie who seldom took no for an answer. Michael had already had a few encounters with her on the phone and discovered she masked an iron will with sweet talk.

Sean, however, was a recently married firefighter, an active man who would have chafed at the restrictions on his life, just as Michael did. Maybe that was the reason that Sean couldn't seem to hide his sympathy each time he saw Michael in this damnable wheelchair. They probably needed to talk about it, but neither one of them had gotten up the nerve. Besides, what was there to say?

"I still don't know how I let you all talk me into moving back to Boston," Michael grumbled as he waved off Ryan's offer of help and struggled to move from the wheelchair to the sofa on his own. "There must be a foot of snow out there. In San Diego, I could be basking in the sunshine beside a pool."

"But you wouldn't be," Ryan said wryly. "The way I hear it, you hadn't set foot outside since you left the hospital."

Michael scowled. His brother clearly had too much information about his habits. There were only a handful of people who could have given it to him, most of them men Michael could have sworn were totally loyal to him.

"Who ratted me out?" he inquired testily.

Ryan held up his hands. "I've been sworn to secrecy. Your men seem to think you have a particularly nasty temper when crossed."

At least he could still intimidate *somebody,* Michael thought with satisfaction. It was a consolation. He certainly hadn't been able to intimidate Ryan's wife, Maggie, though.

Maggie was the one who'd called every single, blessed day pestering him to come East. She'd ignored his cranky responses, talked right over his blistering tirades and pretty much won him over with her silky sweet threats. He wondered if Ryan knew what a weapon he had living with him. Michael was convinced that Maggie Devaney could take over a small country if she was of a mind to. Michael could hardly wait to meet her in person, though he'd prefer to be in top-notch form when he did.

"Why didn't your wife come to the airport with you?" he asked his brother.

"She thought you might like a little time to yourself to get used to things," Ryan said. "She did send along a list of therapists for you to consider. She said you'd been discussing it, but hadn't agreed to hire one yet."

Michael frowned at the understatement. "Actually, what I told her was that I wasn't interested. I could have sworn I'd made that clear."

"You're content to spend the rest of your life in that wheelchair?" Ryan asked mildly.

"The doctors are the ones who consigned me to a wheelchair," Michael responded bitterly. The shattered bone in his thigh had taken two additional surgeries, and the doctors still weren't convinced it would ever heal properly. His knee was artificial. He felt like the Bionic Man, only one who'd gotten faulty parts.

Even if everything healed and worked, he'd never have the agility to return to the kind of work he loved. His navy career was definitely over. He'd declined the offer to push papers behind some desk at the Pentagon. Michael shuddered at the very thought—he'd rather eat raw squid. So he was twenty-seven and out of work and out of hope. He'd learn to live with it…eventually.

Ryan leveled an uncompromising look straight at him. "Is that so? You're blaming this on the doctors? The way I hear it—"

"You apparently hear too damned much," Michael retorted. "Has it occurred to you that I was doing just fine before you and Sean—and your wives—came busting back into my life? I don't need you meddling now. If I decide to stay in Boston, I won't have all of you making me some sort of project." He leveled a daunting look of his own. "Are we clear on that?"

"No project," Ryan echoed dutifully.

Michael studied his brother with a narrowed gaze. That had gone a little too easily, he thought just as the doorbell rang. He scowled at Ryan. "You invite somebody else over?"

Ryan looked just the teensiest bit guilty. "It could be Maggie."

"I thought you said she was giving me some space."

Ryan shrugged. "Well, that's the thing with Maggie. She has her own ideas about how much space a man should have.''

"Great. That's just great.'' Michael eyed his wheelchair with frustration. No way in hell could he haul himself back into the thing and get out of the room before Ryan opened the door. As curious as he was to see the woman who'd married his oldest brother, he wasn't ready for the meeting to take place today. Unfortunately, there was nothing he could do about it. He resigned himself to an early introduction to his sister-in-law.

Before he could catch his breath, Maggie burst into the room, her cheeks red, her eyes flashing and her hair like something from a painting of an auburn-haired goddess. No wonder his brother had fallen for her. Michael was half in love himself, but that was before he caught sight of the curly-haired toddler clutching her hand.

"This is Maggie,'' Ryan said unnecessarily. "And the pint-size replica is Caitlyn. She's just learned to walk, and she has only one speed—full throttle.''

The warning came too late. Caitlyn took one look at Michael, broke free of her mother's grasp and hurtled straight toward him on her chubby, wobbly legs. She was about to grab his injured leg in her powerful little grasp when Michael instinctively bent forward and scooped her up.

Wide green eyes stared at him in shock. He expected immediate tears, but instead a slow smile blossomed on her little face, and he was an instant goner. He'd never realized a kid could steal a person's heart in less than ten seconds flat.

He sat her on his good leg. "Hiya, Caitlyn. I'm your Uncle Mike.''

She studied him intently, then lifted a hand and patted his cheek.

"She's not saying too much yet," Maggie said, "but trust me, she knows how to make herself understood."

"Yeah, I can see that," Michael said, already thoroughly under little Caitlyn's spell.

"Think you can handle her for five minutes?" Maggie asked. "I have groceries in the car. I'm afraid I overdid it. I could use Ryan's help bringing them in."

"Sure. Miss Caitlyn and I will be fine." He wasn't sure how he knew that. It was just that it was the first time in months that someone wasn't looking at him with pity. His niece's expression was merely curious. He could deal with friendly curiosity, especially from someone who hadn't yet learned how to ask complete and probing questions.

But the instant Ryan and Maggie left, Michael had a sudden attack of nerves. He didn't know a whole lot about kids. He had dim memories of his twin brothers, but he'd been little more than a toddler himself when the family had split up. He'd been the youngest in his foster family. Now both of his foster sisters were married, but so far were childless. A couple of the guys on his SEAL team had children, but Michael had tended to steer clear of the gatherings when they'd been present. He didn't like the feelings of envy that washed through him when he was surrounded by tight-knit families.

"So, kid, what do you like to do?" he asked the toddler who seemed perfectly content to sit cuddled in his arms. "I'll bet you have a doll or two at home. Maybe a stuffed bear."

Caitlyn listened intently, but said nothing.

"Then, again, maybe you're one of those liberated little girls who has cars and trucks," Michael continued. "Your mom strikes me as the kind of woman who'd want you to grow up knowing that you have options."

Apparently he'd said the wrong thing, because Caitlyn suddenly looked around the room and huge tears promptly welled up in her eyes.

"Mama," she wailed loudly. "Mama!"

She sounded as if her little heart was breaking. Feeling desperate, Michael awkwardly patted her back. "Hey, it's okay. Your mama is just outside. She and your daddy will be right back."

That brought on a fresh round of tears. "Da-da-da!"

Michael was at a loss. He was about to panic, when the door swung open and Maggie and Ryan came breezing in. Maggie grinned, set the groceries beside the door and swooped in to pick up the squalling child.

"Hey, baby girl, what's all that noise?" Maggie chided.

Just like that, the wails trailed off and the tears stopped. "Mama," Caitlyn said contentedly, patting Maggie's cheek. Then she turned back to Michael and held out her arms.

Michael couldn't help chuckling. "Fickle little thing, aren't you?" he said as he reached for her. "You're going to grow up and break some man's heart."

"She won't be dating until she's at least thirty," Ryan said emphatically.

"Good plan. I can hardly wait to see how well you

stick to it,'' Michael said. ''Especially since this one obviously has a mind of her own already.''

''Don't laugh. You might be called on to help me chase off the boys,'' his brother informed him.

Michael looked at the little angel who was now snuggled against him, half-asleep. ''Just say the word,'' he said solemnly.

''That reminds me,'' Ryan said, taking a slip of paper from his pocket and handing it to Michael.

''What's this?''

''Maggie's list of therapists. She reminded me just now to be sure and give it to you.''

Michael's gaze narrowed. ''And the connection to your daughter's social life would be?''

''If you're going to help me protect Caitlyn from hormone-driven teenaged boys, you're going to have to be in top form,'' Ryan said. ''You might as well pick one and call. If you don't, Maggie will.''

Michael glanced toward the kitchen where his sister-in-law was busily arranging his groceries and dishes so things would be within reach. He took the list and stuffed it in his pocket without comment.

It was only later, after Ryan, Maggie and Caitlyn had gone, that he took out the paper and glanced at the names. One jumped out at him: Kelly Andrews.

Years ago his best friend, Bryan Andrews, had had a sister named Kelly. Was it possible that this was the same girl? He remembered her as being a cute, shy kid, but by now she would have to be, what? Twenty-four most likely.

Michael had lost touch with Bryan years ago. Maybe he'd track him down and ask if his sister was a physical therapist. Purely as a matter of curiosity. He had no intention of asking some therapist to waste her time on him, not when every doctor he'd seen had said that a full recovery was impossible.

And, he thought with self-derision, anything less meant he might as well be dead.

Kelly Andrews was as nervous as if she'd never worked with a patient before. She stood outside the small cluster of apartments in the freezing cold and tried to gather her courage. No matter how many times she told herself that Michael Devaney was a potential client, nothing more, she couldn't help the rush of emotions that filled her.

Michael had been her first teenage crush. Three years older than she was, he and her brother had been friends throughout high school. Michael had never given her so much as a second glance, not as anything more than Bryan's kid sister, anyway. That hadn't stopped her from weaving her share of fantasies about the quiet, dark-haired boy with the intense, brooding gaze and a body that even at seventeen had been impressively well muscled.

It was Bryan who'd told her about Michael being shot and the doctors' very real conviction that he would never walk, much less work as a SEAL, again. Bryan had come back from his visit with Michael sounding worried that his old friend was going to give up. That concern had communicated itself to Kelly.

"His brothers went out to San Diego and convinced him to come back here to recuperate," Bryan had explained two nights before. "I spoke to Ryan after I saw Michael. He says his brother is going to be needing a lot of physical therapy, but so far Michael has flatly refused to ask anyone for help. He did ask about you, though."

Kelly's heart had taken an unsteady leap. "He did?"

"Apparently your name was on a list Ryan's wife made of prospective therapists." Bryan had regarded her with a knowing look. "You interested? I know how you love a challenge. I also know you always had a thing for Michael."

"I did not," she said, though the flush in her cheeks was probably a dead giveaway that she was lying.

As desperately as she wanted to be the one to be there for Michael now, she had hesitated. "From what you say, it's going to be a long, difficult process. He's going to need someone he trusts. Do you think he'll pay any attention to me? In his mind, I'm probably still your kid sister."

Bryan had grinned. "Sis, you forget, I've seen you in action at the clinic when I've come by to pick you up. You're hard to ignore. So, should I tell his brother you'll take the job, and that you won't let Michael's lousy, uncooperative mood scare you off?"

"Hold it. Back up a minute. You said that before—something about brothers. I thought there were only girls in his family."

"The Havilceks only had girls, but Michael was a foster kid."

"Of course. I knew that," Kelly said, suddenly remembering. "At least, I knew he had a different last name. I guess I never really gave much thought to it, because he didn't seem to. So, these brothers are his biological brothers?"

Bryan had nodded. "He hadn't seen them in years till they turned up in San Diego."

"That must have been a shock."

"It was. They were separated when his parents

bailed on all of them. Michael was only four. He barely remembered them.''

She'd stared at her brother with surprise. ''Is this something you just found out, or did you know it when we were kids?''

He shook his head. ''I knew he was a foster kid. But back then, Michael never talked about how he'd wound up with the Havilceks. Every time I started to ask about his real family, he told me the Havilceks were his real family, the only one that counted.''

The story explained a lot…and added to her fascination with Michael Devaney, a fascination she was going to have to ignore if she was going to do her job the way it needed to be done.

''I'm scheduled at the clinic tomorrow, but tell Ryan I'll go by to see Michael the day after tomorrow,'' she had told her brother. ''Whether I stay, though, is going to have to be up to Michael. I can't force him to do therapy if he's not willing.''

Bryan had grinned at her. ''Since when? I thought you specialized in difficult, uncooperative patients.''

She did, but none of them were Michael Devaney, who'd always left her tongue-tied.

Since that conversation with her brother, she'd had more than twenty-four hours to prepare herself for this meeting, but she was as jittery as if it were the first case she'd ever handled. Today she was only doing an evaluation, working up a therapy schedule and making sure that Michael was going to be comfortable having Bryan's kid sister as his therapist. She was counting on a brisk, polite half-hour visit.

She was not counting on the crash of something against the door when she rang the bell. Nor on the bellow telling her to go the hell away.

Oddly enough, the tantrum steadied her nerves and stiffened her resolve. She had a key in her pocket, passed along to her by Bryan, but when she tested the door, she found it was unlocked. Michael might be furious at the universe, he might be testing her courage, but he wasn't really trying to keep her out, or that door would have been locked tight with the security chain in place.

She plastered a smile on her face, squared her shoulders and called out a cheery greeting as she stepped across the threshold. From his wheelchair across the room, Michael glared at her, but he lowered the vase of flowers he had apparently been intent on heaving in her direction.

"Having a bad morning?" she inquired politely, ignoring the shock that seeing him had on her system. Incapacitated or not, he was still the most gorgeous man she'd ever seen.

"Having a bad life," he snapped back. "If you're smart, you'll turn tail and run."

She grinned, which only seemed to infuriate him more.

"I'm serious, dammit."

"I'm sure you are, but you don't scare me," she said with pure bravado. In truth, what really terrified her was the possibility that he'd force her to leave when he so clearly needed someone with her skills to get him out of that chair and back on his feet.

His scowl deepened. "Why not? I've scared off everybody else."

"How? Have you been waving a gun around?"

"Not likely. I believe they've all been removed from the premises," he said bitterly.

''Good. Then that's one less thing I need to worry about,'' she said. ''Mind if I sit down?''

He shrugged. ''Suit yourself.''

She crossed the room, paused in front of his wheelchair and held out her hand. ''It's good to see you again, Michael. You look great.'' And he did. Despite the exhaustion evident in his eyes, despite his unshaven cheeks, he looked exactly the way she'd remembered him—strong and invincible and sexy as sin. Not even his being in a wheelchair could change that.

For a minute he seemed totally taken aback by her comment, but eventually he clasped her hand in his. To her very deep regret, the contact sent a shock straight through her. She'd been hoping she was past being affected by him, that a girl's crush wouldn't inevitably mean that there would be a woman's attraction. It would make the next few weeks or months a lot easier on both of them if she wasn't fighting unreciprocated feelings of attraction.

''You look good, too,'' he muttered, as if he wasn't all that comfortable with polite chitchat. That much at least hadn't changed. Michael never had been much for small talk. He'd always been direct to the point of bluntness.

''I'm sorry you were hurt,'' she said.

''Not half as sorry as I am.''

''Probably not. So let's see what we can do about getting you back on your feet.''

His already grim expression turned to a glower. ''Look, the doctors have already told me that I'll never work as a SEAL again, so let's not waste your time or mine.''

"And that's the only profession out there for a man with a sharp mind?" she asked.

"It's the only one I care about."

She decided not to waste her breath trying to bully him out of such a ridiculously hardheaded, self-defeating stance. "Okay, then, if you're not motivated to walk again so you can get back to work, what about so you can do a few simple things like going for a walk in the park or maybe going out to get your own groceries? The way I remember it, you're an independent guy. Are you going to be content letting other people manage your life for you?"

He patted the wheelchair. "With a little more practice, I'll be able to get around well enough in this."

Now it was her turn to frown. "And you're ready to accept that?"

"It's not as if I have a real choice. The doctors said—"

She cut him off. "Oh, what do they know?" she asked impatiently. "The Michael I remember would take that as a challenge. Why not prove them wrong?" She looked him straight in the eye. "Or do you have something better you'd like to be doing?"

"I keep busy."

Kelly eyed the computer across the room. A bingo game was on the screen. "I imagine you can earn pocket change playing bingo, but I also imagine you'll be bored to tears in a couple of weeks." She shrugged. "Still, it's your choice. I certainly can't force you to do anything you don't want to do."

"Damn straight," he muttered.

She bit back a smile at the display of defiance. "So, Michael, what's it going to be? Do I go or stay?"

Once again, she'd obviously taken him by surprise

by leaving the decision entirely up to him. He blinked hard, then sighed. "Stay if you want to," he said grudgingly.

She grinned at him. "Okay, then, let's do this my way," she said. "Here's what I'm thinking." She laid out the exercises and the rigorous schedule she'd already devised based on the medical information his brother had shared with her. "What do you think?"

"Do you have a masochistic streak I missed when you were a kid?" he grumbled.

Kelly grinned. "No, but I have what it takes to get you out of that chair."

For the first time since she'd arrived, he actually looked her directly in the eye, then slowly nodded. "You may have, at that."

"Then that's all that really matters, isn't it? I'll see you first thing tomorrow. Be ready to work your butt off, Devaney."

He chuckled. "You're tougher than you used to be, Kelly."

"You'd better believe it," she said. "And I don't have a lot of use for self-pity, so get over it."

"Yes, ma'am," he said with a salute.

She gave a nod of satisfaction. "It's always helpful when the client realizes right off who's in charge. Therapy goes much more smoothly."

"I'll try to keep that in mind."

"Not to worry. I'll make sure of it," she said, winking at him as she closed the door behind her.

She paused outside and leaned against the wall, unsuccessfully fighting the tears she hadn't allowed herself to shed in front of him. She'd put on a damn good show for him, but she'd been shaken. What if she couldn't do what she'd promised? What if she couldn't get him out of that wheelchair and back on his feet?

"Stop it," she muttered. Failure was not an option, not with Michael.

As for getting personally involved with a client, that wasn't an option, either, but she had a horrible feeling it was already too late to stop it.

Chapter Two

"So, how did you and Kelly get along?" Bryan Andrews asked Michael when he stopped by for a beer at the end of the day.

Michael studied his one-time best friend with a narrowed gaze. He still wasn't sure how much he appreciated Bryan's unequivocal recommendation of Kelly for the job as his therapist. "Did she do a tour in the marines I don't know about?"

"Nope."

"I remember her as a sweet kid. She's changed." And that was a massive understatement that didn't even take into account the pale gold hair swept up in a knot that revealed the long, delicate line of her neck, the silky complexion and the woman's body with all the appropriate curves.

"She deals with a lot of cantankerous patients at the rehab clinic. She's had to change," Bryan said.

He gave Michael a warning look. "Give her any grief and you'll have me to contend with, too."

"Trust me, I don't think she needs her protective big brother butting in," Michael told him. "She could take me out in ten seconds flat."

"Are you telling me there's finally a woman who can get the upper hand with you?" Bryan taunted, clearly delighted. "And that it's my baby sister?"

"Only because of my weakened condition," Michael assured him.

"Good to know. Back in high school I used to envy the way you could take 'em or leave 'em. The rest of us were slaves to our hormones, but not you. There wasn't a girl in school who could twist you in knots."

That seemed like a lifetime ago to Michael. He'd had a purpose then, and he'd known that a teenage romance would only get in the way. "I was focused on what I wanted to do with my future. I didn't have time to get serious about any girl."

"That doesn't mean you couldn't have had any one you wanted," Bryan said. "It was great hanging out with you. The girls swarmed around *you,* and *I* ended up dating them."

Michael gave him a wry look. "I hope you're not counting on that happening now. I doubt any woman will give me a second look while I'm in this chair."

"If you ask me, that alone is a great reason to get out of it," Bryan said. "Stick with Kelly. She'll have you whipped into shape in no time." His expression sobered. "Seriously, pal, she's good. Cooperate with her. Let her do her thing. If anyone can help you, she can."

"Stop trying to sell her. She has the job. And it's not as if she's going to give me much choice about cooperating,'' Michael retorted, able to laugh for the first time in weeks as he thought of the way Kelly had held her own in the face of his display of temper.

Even as the unfamiliar sound of his laughter filled his cramped apartment, he realized that Kelly Andrews had brought two things into his life during her one brief visit—a breath of fresh air and, far more important, the first faint ray of hope he'd felt since his SEAL team had dragged him out of harm's way.

He immediately brought himself up short. He had been in some tricky, dangerous situations over the years, but nothing had ever scared him quite so badly as the sudden realization, that well-intentioned or not, Kelly might be holding out false hope.

Fear crawled up the back of his throat until he could almost taste it. If he tried to walk and failed, it might be far more devastating than never having tried at all. In the real world, how many miracles was one man entitled to? He'd gotten out of his last mission alive. Maybe that was his quota of good luck for one lifetime.

He looked up and saw that Bryan was regarding him with concern.

"You okay?" Bryan asked.

"Just reminding myself of something," he said grimly.

"Judging from that expression on your face, it wasn't anything good."

Michael shrugged. He wasn't about to tell Kelly's brother that he'd been reminding himself that she was a mere woman, not a miracle worker. It was a distinction he couldn't allow himself to forget, not for one single second.

* * *

"Are you sure you ought to be taking on this particular client?" Moira Brady asked Kelly, her expression filled with concern.

"I'm a professional. I can keep my feelings under control," Kelly insisted. "Besides, it's been years since I had my crush on Michael Devaney. I was a kid."

Moira regarded her skeptically. "Then you had absolutely no reaction to seeing him again? He was just a patient, someone you happened to know from years ago?"

"Absolutely."

"Liar."

Kelly frowned at her best friend, who also ran the rehabilitation clinic where Kelly worked part-time on days when she didn't have private patients scheduled. "I don't understand why you're making such a big deal about this, Moira."

"Because I don't want to see you get hurt," Moira said bluntly. "You always give your patients a hundred and ten percent, Kelly. You care about their progress. You feel guilty if they don't achieve the results you've been anticipating."

"Well, of course I do. Are you saying I shouldn't?"

"No, but add in your personal history with Michael Devaney, and I see a disaster waiting to happen."

"Oh, please," Kelly said derisively. "Michael and I don't have a personal history."

"But you fantasized about one," Moira countered. "I know that because you told me about him in glowing detail way back when we first met in college. He'd been gone for three years by then, but you hadn't forgotten the least little thing about him. Can you honestly tell me that there wasn't one teeny-tiny spark when you walked into his apartment yesterday?"

A spark? More like a bonfire, Kelly thought wryly. Not that she intended to admit it. "No spark," she said flatly.

Moira's gaze narrowed suspiciously. "Okay, is this one of those semantics things? What if I asked about fireworks? Would you admit to that?"

Kelly sighed. "It doesn't matter. Michael Devaney doesn't think of me in that way. I'm his friend's kid sister."

"Think he'll remember that when you're massaging his muscles?"

Kelly felt the heat climbing into her cheeks. She'd been wondering about that very thing herself. Anticipating it. She'd been itching to get her hands on those taut muscles of Michael's for years. Now she had the perfect excuse. She swallowed hard and banished the totally unprofessional thought.

Scowling, she reminded both of them, "I'm a professional, dammit!"

"Yeah, sure," Moira said. "You keep telling yourself that. And just in case you forget it, I'll mention it to you every chance I get."

Michael couldn't seem to get his pants on. Lately he'd taken to wearing sweatpants because they were easy and comfortable and warm, but he'd gotten it into his head to put on a pair of jeans for this first session with Kelly. His bum leg wasn't cooperating.

He had the pants half on and half off when the doorbell rang. Scowling, he gave one more forceful yank on the jeans and barely managed to stifle a howl of agony. Or at least he thought he had, until he looked straight up into Kelly's worried gray eyes. Her cheeks were flushed and she was still wearing a bright pink ski jacket over a sweater that looked so soft he immediately wanted to stroke his hand over the material…and the woman under it.

"Are you okay?" she asked.

"Aside from having an uninvited guest appear in my bedroom, I'm just peachy," he growled.

Her chin shot up and fire blazed in her eyes. "Not uninvited. I'm here for our appointment, and I'm not even a minute early. I only came in because you didn't answer the door and I thought I heard you cry out."

"I didn't answer the door because I wasn't dressed," he retorted. "How the hell did you get in, anyway?"

"Your brother gave me a key," she said. "And since you're obviously okay, I'll head on into the living room and get set up. You might as well strip out of those pants before you join me."

The suggestion probably couldn't have been more innocent, but something that felt a whole lot like desire slammed straight through him. "I beg your pardon?"

Kelly gestured toward his jeans. "The pants. Lose them. I'm going to start with a massage to loosen up those tight muscles."

Michael swallowed hard. She intended to put her hands all over him? He frowned at her. "Did we talk about that when you were here yesterday?"

"I'm sure it came up," she said briskly. "Five minutes, okay? I have another client in an hour, so there's no time to waste."

Michael stared after her as she left his room. They

most definitely had not talked about this. He would never have agreed to letting her put her soft as silk hands on his body. He might be injured, but he wasn't dead. One touch and he suspected this could go from a therapy session to something else entirely. It had been too blasted long since he'd felt a woman's hands on his bare skin. His best friend's baby sister was not the woman who should be testing his willpower.

Still wearing his jeans—zipped up and securely in place now—he wheeled himself into the living room. "We need to rethink this," he said tightly. "It's not going to work out."

She leveled a look straight at him. "Oh? Why is that?"

"I don't think you ought to be touching me."

He could almost swear that her lips twitched at that, but she managed to cling to a perfectly serious expression.

Hands shoved into the pockets of her own snug-fitting jeans, she inquired curiously, "I don't make you nervous, do I?"

"Of course you make me nervous," he retorted. "What man wouldn't be nervous when an attractive woman he barely knows suddenly announces that she's going to be massaging him?"

"You've known me since I was fourteen," she reminded him. "And it's therapy, not seduction."

"Tell that to my body," he mumbled under his breath, very aware that the conversation alone was having an extremely interesting effect on certain parts of his anatomy. This was Kelly, dammit. What was wrong with him? Bryan would mop the floor with him—and rightly so—if he heard about Michael's reaction to his sister.

"What was that?" she inquired, her expression all innocence.

"Nothing."

"Come on, Michael. You were a SEAL. The way I hear it, they're the bravest of the brave. Are you actually going to fire me before we even get started, just because I'm going to massage you? What would your buddies think of that?"

The challenge hung in the air. The woman was good. Really good. She knew exactly how to play him. He scowled at her. "If I had half a brain, I would."

She did grin then. "Is that a yes or a no?"

Michael considered his options. He could fire her right now and hire somebody else—preferably some ox of a man—or he could try getting through at least one treatment before calling it quits. He owed Kelly for one session anyway, and something told him she wouldn't take a cent if he didn't let her do her job. He weighed fairness against self-preservation, and opted for fairness.

"We'll see how it goes today," he said finally.

She gave the slightest little nod of satisfaction. "Okay, then, let me help you out of those pants."

One fierce look from him stopped her in her tracks. "Or you can get them yourself," she said.

Wincing at the shooting pain that accompanied every movement, Michael finally managed to shed the pants and heave himself onto her portable massage table. At least he was on his stomach, so he wouldn't have to see her face when she saw the jagged scars from the surgery. He didn't miss her sharp intake of breath, though.

He felt a soft splash of warm oil on his injured leg,

then the skimming touch of her hands as she smoothed it down the back of his thigh and over his calf. Her touch was gentle rather than provocative, but that didn't stop the sudden shock of awareness that flowed through him. Michael forced his mind to detach itself from her actions and concentrate on counting backward from a thousand. It was a tactic that had served him well in other situations involving slow torture.

"Am I hurting you?" she asked.

The simple question dragged her from the periphery of his consciousness right back into his head. "No," he said tersely, trying to mentally haul himself back to that nice, safe place.

For a few moments, blessed silence fell. Michael made it all the way down to nine hundred and two before she spoke again.

"What happened?" she asked.

He resigned himself to staying in the disconcerting moment. "When?"

"When you were hurt."

"I walked into a trap," he said, still filled with self-loathing at the stupidity of it. He should have known what was going on. He should never have trusted the intelligence report that the caves had been cleared of terrorists. He'd always relied on his own surveillance, his own instincts, but this one time he'd gotten anxious, a little careless. It was a bitter lesson that would have served him well in the future...if only he had one.

"Where were you?"

Too many years of keeping silent about his work kept him cautious even now. "I can't say."

"But you were a Navy SEAL, right? So I can assume that this had something to do with the war on terrorism?''

''You can assume anything you want to assume.''

Her fingers began to massage a little deeper, working muscles too long unused. Knots of tension in his legs seemed to ease, at least as long as she didn't venture too close to the scars. That area was still amazingly tender. He yelped the first time she touched the bullet's exit wound on the back of his thigh.

''Sorry.''

''I'll survive.''

''I'm sure of that,'' she agreed. ''But I'll be more careful around the scars. I can't ignore them, though, because that skin's going to need to be stretched.''

''Whatever you say.''

She patted his leg. ''That's it for today, then.''

He glanced up and regarded her with surprise. ''You're finished?''

''It's been nearly an hour, and I have another appointment across town.''

''At this rate, we're not going to make much progress,'' he said, suddenly disgruntled by the too-quick end of the session and the complete lack of anything remotely like measurable improvement. ''I thought you were going to work my butt off, or am I misquoting you?''

''Nope, that's what I said, and that day will come. I've got you scheduled for two hours, day after tomorrow. We'll start the exercises then.'' She met his gaze. ''That is, if I passed today's probation.''

He ought to tell her to get the hell out and stay away, but he couldn't seem to make himself do it. He was too afraid of the disappointment or disdain he'd see in her eyes. Either one would make him feel like a jerk. Besides, a part of him couldn't help clinging to the possibility that she was his best hope for getting back on his feet again.

He met her gaze. Now that he was willing to give therapy a try, he wanted to see progress. He wasn't scared of a little pain or hard work. In fact, he looked forward to it. "Make it three hours, day after tomorrow."

"You're not ready for three hours," she said flatly.

He scowled at her reaction. "Let me be the judge of what I can handle. I've gone through training so rigorous, it would make your therapy seem like child's play."

"Have you done it since having several bones shattered, to say nothing of going through—what was it—three surgeries?" she inquired tartly.

The woman was tough as nails. It was a trait he couldn't help admiring. "Okay, you made your point. Two hours, but if I'm up to it, we'll go to three the next time," he bargained. "Is it a deal?"

Kelly looked for a moment as if she might argue. Finally she held out her hand. "Deal."

Michael took her hand in his and instantly regretted it. It had taken every ounce of willpower he possessed to ignore the way her hands had moved over his body earlier. Now, with something as simple as a handshake, he was once more thoroughly aware of her as a desirable woman.

Her skin was amazingly soft, her grip strong. A faint hint of the aromatic oil she'd used for the massage lingered in the air. It wasn't the least bit feminine—quite the opposite, in fact—but it suddenly turned erotic. If he'd been another kind of man in a different situation, he would have brought her hand to his lips and brushed a kiss across her knuckles. Instead, he released her hand as if he'd been burned.

A faint flicker of surprise flashed across her face, followed almost instantly by understanding. To his disgust she'd apparently guessed that for one brief second he'd let himself cross some sort of line.

"Is there anything I can do for you before I go?" she asked.

A thousand and one wicked possibilities slammed through him. "Not a thing," he said tightly.

"Are you sure?"

"I thought you were in a hurry."

"I can spare five minutes," she said, regarding him with amusement. "I could fix you some breakfast if you haven't had any."

Forget breakfast, and five minutes wouldn't be nearly long enough to act on a single one of those wicked possibilities, Michael thought wryly. He wondered what she would do, though, if he suggested, say, a kiss.

It wasn't propriety or the thought of Bryan pounding him to a pulp that stopped him. It was the very distinct likelihood that it would backfire on him. If he was already having totally inappropriate thoughts about Kelly after one very brief therapy session, a kiss could very well send him over the edge. He might start obsessing about the way she'd feel in his arms. He might forget all about the reason she was there… to help him get back on his feet, not to help him prove he was still first and foremost a man.

Michael sighed heavily, determined to ignore the tantalizing sparks sizzling in the air. "I'll see you day after tomorrow."

She almost looked disappointed. "Whatever you say."

To keep himself from doing anything foolish, he deliberately turned his wheelchair in the direction of the kitchen, putting his back to her. "Lock the door on your way out," he said.

He expected to hear the door open and close, the lock click into place. Instead, there was nothing, not even a whisper of movement.

"What are you going to do with the rest of your day?" she asked finally.

"Planning my activities is not part of your job," he retorted more sharply than necessary.

"I was asking, not planning," she responded, evidently undaunted by his tone. "I hate to think of you being shut away in here all alone."

"You might not think my company has much to recommend it," he said. "But I'm content with it."

"Have you called the Havilceks and told them you're back? Have you even told them what happened to you?"

Back still to Kelly, Michael frowned at the question. He'd made one call to them from San Diego to let them know he'd been injured, but that he was recuperating. To his astonishment, Mrs. Havilcek had wanted to fly out right away, but he'd explained about Ryan and Sean being there.

"Oh, Michael, that's wonderful," she'd said with what sounded like total sincerity. "I won't come now, then, but you call me if you need me. I can be there the next day."

The memory of that promise had been enough to warm him whenever loneliness had crept in after Ryan and Sean had headed back East. It was enough to know that Mrs. Havilcek would come if called, and amazing to think that after all the years she'd cared for and loved him, that he'd even doubted for a minute that she would.

"Have you gotten in touch with them?" Kelly prodded.

"Not since I got to Boston," he admitted.

She regarded him incredulously. "Why on earth not?"

He wasn't sure he could explain it. He loved his foster family. The Havilceks had been great parents to him. And he couldn't have been any closer to the girls if they had been his real big sisters. But when Ryan and Sean had turned up, he'd felt almost disloyal to the Havilceks, as if having feelings for his biological brothers was some sort of betrayal of all his foster family had done for him. He was still wrestling with how to handle keeping all of them in their rightful place in his life, a life that had changed dramatically since he'd last seen them.

"I'll call them," he told Kelly, "once things are a little more settled."

"You mean after you're back on your feet? Don't you want them to see you when you're not a hundred percent? Do you think they'd care about that?" she demanded indignantly.

He found the suggestion that he was acting out of misplaced pride vaguely insulting. "No, of course not. It's not about that at all."

"What then?"

He regarded her with a wry expression. "You know, Kelly, maybe there's something we ought to get straight. You're here to help me walk again. Leave the rest of my life to me."

"I would, if you weren't so obviously dead set on wasting it," she shot back. "But that's okay. I'll drop it for now."

"For good," he countered.

She flashed him a brilliant smile. "Sorry. I can't promise that."

Before he could threaten to fire her if she insisted on meddling in things that were none of her concern, she was out the door. The lock clicked softly into place, just as he'd requested.

Michael should have felt relieved to have her gone, relieved to be alone with hours stretching out ahead of him to do whatever struck his fancy, at least given the limits of his mobility.

Instead, all he felt was regret.

Chapter Three

If Michael had been anticipating a lonely, boring day to himself after Kelly's departure, he should have known better. Despite his admonition to Ryan that he was to be no one's project, his brothers and sisters-in-law were apparently determined that he not have a single minute to himself to sit and brood. In fact, by the end of the day he wouldn't have been surprised to discover a schedule of their assigned comings and goings posted outside his door.

Maggie was first on the scene, with Caitlyn in tow. His niece came in dragging a purple suitcase on wheels, which he discovered was filled with her favorite picture books and a doll that was apparently capable of saying all the words Caitlyn had yet to master. She shoved the doll in his arms, then climbed up beside him on the sofa, put a book in his lap and regarded him expectantly.

"She wants you to read to her," Maggie said, as if that hadn't been perfectly obvious, even to a novice uncle like him.

Michael studied the thick board book with its brightly colored pictures, started to flip it open to the first page, only to have Caitlyn very firmly turn it back to the cover and point emphatically. He gathered he was supposed to begin with the title.

"The Runaway Bunny," he began.

Caitlyn nodded happily, then snuggled closer.

Michael glanced in Maggie's direction, caught her satisfied smile and gave in to the inevitable. He discovered that reading to a one-year-old might not involve complex plots, but it had its own rewards. Caitlyn was a very appreciative audience, clapping her little hands together with enthusiasm and giggling merrily.

Even so, after five books, he was more than ready for a break. He uttered a sigh of relief when Maggie announced that lunch was ready. He prayed it would be accompanied by a good stiff drink, but since he hadn't found a drop of liquor in his cabinets after Maggie had stocked them, he wasn't holding out much hope.

"Shall I bring lunch in there?" she asked.

"Nope. I'll come to the kitchen," he responded. He glanced at Caitlyn. "How about it? Want to hitch a ride with Uncle Mike?"

She nodded happily and held out her arms.

"Whoa, sweet pea. Let me get settled first." He struggled into the wheelchair, then lifted her to his lap and wheeled into the kitchen, where Maggie was pointedly ignoring the fact that it had taken a much longer time for them to get there than it would have taken for her to bring the lunch into the living room to him and Caitlyn.

"How did your first therapy session go?" she asked as she served the thick sandwiches and potato salad she'd prepared.

"Why am I not surprised that you knew it was this morning?" he inquired dryly. "And why am I stunned that it took you this long to get around to asking about it?"

Maggie gave him an irrepressible smile. "I'm learning restraint."

Michael laughed. "How's it going?"

"Pretty well today, apparently." Her expression sobered. "So, how *did* it go? You didn't scare Kelly off, did you? She seemed like a nice young woman when she came by the pub to pick up a key to this place from Ryan."

"About that," he began, intending to explain that his key wasn't to be handed out at random to anyone who asked or professed a need for a copy.

Maggie held up a silencing hand. "I know. I told Ryan he should have consulted with you first, but he was afraid she'd show up for the consultation and you wouldn't let her in. He figured the key would assure that you'd see her at least once." She met his gaze. "You can always ask her to give it back. Did you?"

"No," he admitted, not entirely sure why he hadn't. Maybe it was best not to examine his reasons.

Maggie seemed to be struggling with a grin. "I see. Then things have gone okay with Kelly?"

He was not about to admit that Kelly had actually left today before he was ready for her to go. Maggie would clearly make way too much of that, though whether she'd deduce it was enthusiasm for therapy or for the therapist was a toss-up.

"She'll be back day after tomorrow," he conceded grudgingly, and let it go at that.

"Terrific."

He studied his sister-in-law intently. "So, Maggie, who has the afternoon shift?"

She regarded him blankly. "Excuse me?"

"Is Sean coming by to take over when you take the peanut here home for her nap? Or maybe his wife? Then, again, Deanna has already called in today, so maybe it's Ryan's turn."

Color bloomed in Maggie's cheeks.

Michael sighed. "I thought so. You all divvied up the assignment so I wouldn't be alone for more than an hour or so at a time, didn't you? I'm amazed nobody took the night shift, or is somebody that I don't know about sitting in the hallway from midnight to seven in the morning?"

Maggie's chin rose, eyes flashing. "Your brothers are concerned about you. It's perfectly natural."

"Where was that concern twenty years ago? Or even five years ago?" he demanded heatedly. "Hovering now won't make up for all those years they didn't do a damn thing to find me."

Maggie regarded him in silence.

"No answer for that?" he pushed, even though he knew he was being totally unreasonable by taking years of pent-up anger out on her. "I didn't think so."

Before he could wheel himself away from the table, Maggie rested her hand on his. "They were hurt, too, you know."

"Not by me, dammit!"

"No, of course not. But you were all kids," she

reminded him with gentle censure. "None of you could have been expected to fight the system to find your way back to the others."

"We've all been adults for a long time now," he retorted.

She regarded him with an unflinching stare. "Then I'll ask you this—did you look for Ryan or Sean?"

Michael's heart throbbed dully as he thought of how hard he'd worked to block out all memories of his big brothers. He'd substituted the loving Havilceks for his family. They would never have turned their backs on one of their kids, not even him, though he'd spent a lot of years with his heart in his throat expecting the worst.

"No," he admitted, "but—"

"Can't you let it be enough that your brothers are back in your life now? We're family, Michael. It may be late, but let's not waste any more time by tossing around a lot of useless recriminations."

Gazing into his sister-in-law's troubled green eyes, Michael fought off the desire to prolong the argument. Maggie was right. There was nothing to be gained by holding grudges, and maybe quite a lot to be gained by forgiveness.

"Okay, then," he said at last. "I'll work on putting aside the past, if you'll do something for me in return."

"Anything," she agreed readily.

"Can the hovering," he said bluntly. "I have to learn to do things for myself. And if there's something I can't manage, I'll call and ask for help."

She studied him skeptically. "You promise that you won't shut us out completely?"

He grinned at that. "As if you'd let me. No, Maggie, I won't shut any of you out. You're welcome here anytime…just not *all* the time.''

She laughed. ''Okay, I get it. I'll speak to Ryan, Sean and Deanna.''

''Thank you.''

''You're welcome. Of course, that puts you in my debt, at least a little, doesn't it?''

He eyed her warily. ''A little, I suppose. Why?''

''Will you come to the pub on Friday night? There will be Irish music, and the special's fish and chips. Ryan can come by to pick you up.''

Michael was surprised to find that the prospect held some appeal. ''You're a tough negotiator, Maggie Devaney.''

''I know,'' she said with unmistakable pride. ''I had to be to win your brother's heart. You may find this hard to believe, but he was even less trusting than you are.''

''You're right. I do find that hard to believe.''

''Well, it's true.'' She smiled at him. ''Will you come?''

''I'll come,'' he agreed. ''But I'll get there on my own.''

She opened her mouth, but he cut her off before she could protest. ''If I can't manage it, I'll call.''

''Fair enough, then. I'll do these dishes and get out of your hair.''

Michael glanced at his niece and saw that she was nodding off in her booster seat at the table. ''I think maybe you ought to get Caitlyn home for her nap, instead. I can clear things away in here.''

''But—''

He deliberately scowled at her. ''Go, Maggie, before you undo all the warm and fuzzy feelings I'm developing toward you.''

She laughed at that, picked up her daughter, then bent and kissed his cheek. ''I'm glad to have you as part of our family. You'll get to meet the rest of the O'Briens on Friday night. You might want to brace yourself. My family can be a little overwhelming. Ryan and I have been married for nearly two years now, and they still make *him* nervous.''

''Now there's a fine recommendation,'' Michael responded dryly. ''I'm really looking forward to Friday night, after that.''

''The music will compensate for the chaos. I promise.''

Michael believed her, which was a bit of a miracle in and of itself. Other than the men on his SEAL team, he'd long ago lost his faith in promises.

Kelly wasn't sure what to expect when she arrived for her second therapy session with Michael. Even though during her last visit he'd agreed to continue with his rehabilitation, he wouldn't be the first patient to have a change of heart between sessions, especially if he'd spent the intervening hours brooding.

She rang the bell at his apartment promptly at 10:00 a.m., then waited to see what sort of greeting she got. She counted it a positive sign when nothing crashed against the door. Nor were there any cries of pain from inside. So far, it was going better than either of her earlier visits.

When another full minute had passed, she rang the bell again. ''Michael, it's me. Is everything okay? Should I come on in?''

More silence. She frowned at the door. Had he

bailed on her, after all? Or was he inside, simply ignoring her, hoping she would go away? She was about to put her key in the lock, when the front door of the building crashed open. Kelly whirled around and found herself staring straight into Michael's very blue eyes.

"Sorry," he said as he awkwardly tried to manipulate the chair into the foyer. "I had to go out. I thought I'd be back before you got here, but everything took longer than I expected."

Kelly stared at him. "You went out?" she said blankly. Where? How? She resisted the urge to ask questions he would no doubt find intrusive, if not downright insulting.

"To the store," he said, holding up two small plastic bags crammed with groceries. He looked astonishingly pleased with himself.

"How did you manage?" she asked. "Did you call a taxi?"

"Of course not. The store's only a few blocks away."

Her incredulity grew. "You went in your wheelchair?"

"I sure as hell didn't walk," he retorted, his good mood evaporating.

Kelly immediately felt guilty for spoiling his moment of triumph. "Sorry. I just wasn't expecting it. It's terrific that you were able to manage on your own."

His scowl stayed firmly in place. "You're not out of a job just yet, if that's what's worrying you."

"No, of course not. You caught me off guard, that's all." She gestured toward the apartment. "And I was worried when you didn't answer the door."

"Well, I'm here now, and that clock of yours is no doubt ticking, so let's get started."

Filled with regret about the tension she'd managed to cause, she merely nodded and stepped aside. "Go on in. I'll be right behind you."

He wheeled past without comment. Kelly leaned against the wall for a second and drew in a deep breath. Why was it that she couldn't manage to have one single encounter with this man without some sort of misunderstanding? She'd never had problems making herself clear before, but Michael managed to keep her off-kilter and tongue-tied. When she finally did speak, everything kept coming out wrong. Sure, he was understandably prickly, but she seemed to have a special knack for setting him off.

Determined not to let it happen again, she squared her shoulders and carried her equipment inside. While Michael was putting his groceries away, she got set up.

A few minutes later he came into the living room wearing a pair of boxers, a T-shirt and a frown. He gestured toward the massage table.

"Are we starting with that again?"

Kelly nodded.

He struggled awkwardly from the chair to the table, then stretched out facedown. Kelly put some of her aromatic oil on his injured leg and began to massage, trying to ignore the body heat the man put out. If she were ever stranded outdoors in a blizzard, Michael was definitely the man she'd want with her. He emitted heat like a blast furnace.

His muscles were also knotted with tension, probably due in part to her. She smoothed her hands over his powerful thigh and down the length of his calf until she finally felt the tension begin to ease.

The massage probably went on longer than necessary because she enjoyed touching him so much, enjoyed the fact that for once they weren't at odds, enjoyed even more the soft sigh of pleasure that eased through him.

It was the sigh, though, that snapped her back to reality and reminded her that the massage was not about her enjoyment, or even his. It was therapy, a prelude to some of the stretching exercises she'd scheduled for today. Kelly had a feeling that one reason she'd put off getting to those was the knowledge that Michael was going to be indignant that she wasn't assigning him anything more strenuous.

"Okay, that's it," she forced herself to say finally.

Michael sat up slowly and regarded her with confusion. "For the day? We're finished?"

She smiled at his obvious dismay. "Not just yet. I have some stretching exercises for you to try. It'll help with getting those torn muscles and ligaments back into shape."

As she'd expected, he frowned.

"Stretching?" he asked disdainfully. "Come on, Kelly, can't we move beyond that?"

She regarded him evenly. "You straighten that injured leg out and do ten leg lifts and we'll reevaluate my plan."

"Piece of cake," he boasted.

"Okay, then, let's see it," she said, her arms folded across her chest as she stood back and waited.

She wasn't the least bit surprised when he couldn't get his leg to straighten completely. Nor when his first attempt to lift it in the air had sweat beading on his brow. He was wincing in obvious pain as he finally managed to raise the leg a scant three or four inches.

"Okay, you win," he grumbled, scowling fiercely. "But nobody likes a know-it-all woman, you know."

"I don't need you to like me," she said cheerfully. "I just need you to trust me."

"Sweetheart, there are very few people on earth I trust," he said bitterly. "I don't know you well enough for you to make the cut."

The comment tore straight through her, but she forced herself not to let it show. "Then maybe we need to do something to change that."

His gaze narrowed. "Such as?"

"Spend some time together."

Her response clearly startled him.

"You're asking me out?" he inquired warily.

Kelly's pulse skittered crazily at the idea, but she kept her tone even. "As if I'd date an ill-tempered old man like you," she taunted.

He frowned at that. "I'm only three years older than you."

She grinned. "I notice you didn't try to argue with the ill-tempered part."

He shrugged. "Didn't see much point in it. When you're right, you're right. I'll try to stop taking my bad moods out on you."

"Thank you."

"So, if you weren't suggesting a date, what were you suggesting?"

"Just getting out in the world. It'll give me a chance to evaluate your motor skills in a more realistic setting, and you can ask me whatever questions are on your mind."

He regarded her doubtfully. "And you think that will build trust?"

"Couldn't hurt," she said.

"What do you think your brother will have to say about you and me going out?"

"Bryan doesn't interfere in my work. For that matter, though, he's welcome to come along." Maybe her brother could smooth things over between them, keep her from saying the wrong thing, or at the very least, keep Michael from misinterpreting what she said and taking offense. "Is it a deal?"

He seemed to be struggling with the offer, weighing it from every angle to see if he could find a catch. Kelly could almost see the wheels in his head turning. She realized then that this whole trust business was a far larger issue than she'd first assumed. Obviously it had to do with his family background. How on earth could she be expected to overcome that kind of distrust in a few short therapy sessions?

She looked him in the eye. "Or would you prefer to start over with another therapist."

"No," he said at once.

She might have found the quick response flattering if she didn't suspect it had more to do with his dread of wasting time searching for someone new than it did with her.

"Okay, then," she said. "Pick a day and we'll get together."

"Friday," he suggested finally. "I promised my sister-in-law today that I'd go to the pub Friday evening. Why don't you and Bryan come along?"

Kelly nodded. "Sounds good. Want us to pick you up? You're on our way."

"Sure," he said eventually, as if he'd wrestled with that decision, too.

She grinned at him. "You're not sacrificing your independence, you know. You really are on our way."

He gave her a self-deprecating grin that made Kelly's heart flip over.

"I know," he admitted. "That's why I finally gave in. I'm stubborn. I'm not an idiot."

She laughed then. "A distinction I'll try to remember."

His expression sobered. "So will I. I really am sorry for giving you such a rough time. It's just that all this is so blasted frustrating."

She patted his hand. "Compared to some people I've worked with, you're downright sweet-natured."

Michael winced at the description, just as she'd expected him to.

"Don't worry," she reassured him. "I won't let it get around. I imagine you big, tough SEALs pride yourselves on being as cantankerous as they come."

"You'd better believe it," he agreed, his fierce expression belied by the twinkle in his eyes. After an instant, the sparkle dimmed. "Of course, *ex*-SEALs are another breed entirely."

There was no mistaking the return of bitterness and despair in his tone. Kelly desperately wanted to make things better, but she wasn't sure if she could find the right words. She made herself try, though.

"You know, Michael, it seems to me that in some ways it takes as much bravery to face a future all alone without the SEALs as it does to take on some dangerous, covert mission surrounded by an entire team of highly trained experts," she told him.

"In other words, if I don't get over myself and face

this whole therapy thing head-on, I'm a coward?'' he asked.

''Your words, not mine,'' she said.

He sighed heavily. ''Then maybe that's exactly what I am,'' he conceded, his expression bleak. ''Because if I'm no longer a SEAL, then I don't know who the hell I am.''

Kelly could have offered a whole string of platitudes that would have meant nothing at all to him, but she didn't. Instead, she merely touched his shoulder. ''But you'll figure it out,'' she said quietly.

''I wish I were as sure of that as you seem to be.''

''You're a smart man, you'll find your way,'' she insisted. ''Trust me.''

His gaze captured hers and held. ''Which brings us full circle.''

She gathered up her things and headed for the door. ''I'll see you Friday night and we'll work on it,'' she said, because suddenly there was nothing on earth more important to her than gaining Michael Devaney's trust…unless it was giving him back his faith in himself.

Chapter Four

Bryan was staring at Kelly as if she'd suddenly grown two heads. "Tell me again how this came about?" he demanded, when she invited him to join her and Michael at Ryan's Place on Friday night. "You asked Michael—your patient—out on a date? How many rules does that break?"

"None precisely," Kelly retorted defensively. "And it's not a date. Michael admits he has issues with trust. I find it's impossible to do my job if my client doesn't trust my judgment. I thought it might help if he got to know me better as someone other than your baby sister. Apparently he agrees, because he suggested going to Ryan's Place on Friday night. Now do you want to come along or not?"

"Oh, I'm coming," Bryan said, his expression grim. "If only to make sure you don't do anything stupid. You seem to forget that I can read you like a book. It may be an issue of trust for Michael, but it's a whole lot more for you.''

Kelly found her brother's attitude extremely annoying, to say nothing of patronizing. ''I am not going to try to seduce him, if that's what you're worried about,'' she said heatedly.

''What if *he* tries to seduce *you?* Will you take him up on it?'' Bryan asked with the sort of bluntness he normally reserved for the patients he counseled in his psychology practice.

Much as she wanted to believe that Michael attempting to seduce her was a possibility, Kelly was a realist where Michael Devaney was concerned. He was not going to try to get her into bed, not Friday night, most likely not ever. More's the pity.

She regarded her brother with a sour look. ''I'll let you know if the issue arises. Then, again, maybe I won't. It's not really any of your business.''

''How can you say that? Of course it is. I'm your brother, and I'm the one who talked you into taking this job.''

''Oh, for heaven's sake, Bryan, you didn't talk me into anything. You mentioned it. I spoke with Ryan and then consulted with Michael. He and I were the ones who agreed to give it a try. At best, you gave me a lead on a job. You've done it a hundred times before without working yourself into a frenzy over the outcome.''

''But this was different.''

''Why?''

''Because we're talking about Michael,'' he replied with evident impatience. ''I knew you'd jump at the chance to help him because you always had a thing for him.''

She kissed her brother's cheek. "Too late for regrets now, worrywart. I'm a big girl. I can handle this."

"You can handle Michael's therapy," he corrected. "I don't have a doubt in the world about that. But this? This is social. Michael's not thinking straight these days, and neither, apparently, are you. You'll end up getting your heart broken."

She frowned at him. "Thanks for the vote of confidence."

"You know what I mean. I thought for sure you'd be over your crush by now, but you aren't, are you?"

"I was barely a teenager when you first brought Michael home. He was gorgeous. Naturally I was intrigued by him," she said, ignoring the fact that none of those feelings had gone away. She was still very much attracted to Michael, something her big brother definitely didn't need to have confirmed. Maybe it was time to turn the tables, put him on the hot seat. "Now let's talk about your love life—or should I say your lack of one."

His scowl deepened. "Nothing to discuss," he said tightly.

"Oh, really? Then that fling with what's-her-name is really over?" she pressed, in part because she knew of someone else who was ready and willing to take on Bryan, if he'd finally wised up.

"It wasn't a fling," he said defensively. "And you know her name. It's Debra."

"Short for dim-witted," Kelly muttered. "You know, for an intelligent man who has a degree in psychology, you have exceptionally lousy taste in women."

"Thank you for sharing your opinion," her brother

retorted. "Next time you feel so inclined, bite your tongue."

She grinned at him. "Advice you should consider following when it comes to Friday night."

Bryan sighed heavily, picked up his jacket and headed out without saying another word.

Now it was Kelly's turn to sigh. She should have kept her mouth shut about Friday, because if she knew her brother at all—and she did—he was on his way straight to Michael's, probably to warn him to behave or get his teeth knocked down his throat.

Kelly considered calling Michael to warn him, but why bother? Bryan was a great guy, but he definitely leaned more toward intellectual pursuits than physical prowess. Michael could probably use a good laugh. He might be in a wheelchair, but she had a feeling he could still take her brother in a fight. Maybe it would do both of them good for Michael to remember that.

Michael was watching the Celtics game on TV and cursing the fact that there wasn't a beer in the place, when the doorbell rang. Since he'd all but banished his brothers from stopping by uninvited, he figured he shouldn't just tell his visitor that the door was unlocked. He wheeled across the room and found Bryan on his doorstep, a scowl firmly in place and a six-pack in his hand.

"Talk about your mixed messages," Michael said, moving aside to let his friend in.

Bryan stared at him blankly. "What?"

"Hey, you're the psychologist," Michael reminded him. "Shouldn't you understand that arriving with a frown on your face and a peace offering in your hand could be a bit confusing?"

"Was I frowning? Sorry," Bryan said, though the apology sounded halfhearted.

Michael studied him curiously. The Bryan he'd once known had always been upbeat, always able to put a positive spin on things. He could spot the silver linings on the cloudiest days. It was a trait that probably contributed to his skill as a psychologist. Clearly, something had to be weighing mighty heavily on him to put this scowl on his face.

"Something on your mind?" Michael probed cautiously.

"You could say that."

"Why don't you pour a couple of those beers and tell me all about it?" Michael suggested. Listening to somebody else's problems for a change would be good for him, he decided. It might make him forget his own.

While Bryan headed for the kitchen, Michael went back in the living room and muted the sound on the TV. He didn't have to listen to the game, but he wasn't going to skip it. Basketball was the one thing he'd missed when he was off in various godforsaken locations. Of course, he'd also missed playing it, but for now he'd have to settle for the vicarious thrills of watching a good game on TV.

Bryan returned, handed Michael his beer, then sank down on the sofa, still looking worried.

"Woman problems?" Michael asked.

"Not the way you mean. It's Kelly."

Now it was Michael's turn to frown. "Has something happened to your sister? She was here this afternoon, and she seemed perfectly fine."

"Yeah, well, since then, she's apparently lost her mind."

Michael stared at him. "What the hell are you talking about?"

"This whole cockamamy scheme that the two of you should spend time together," Bryan explained. "Whose idea was it?"

"Hers," Michael said at once, still not seeing why Bryan was making such a big deal out of it. "What's wrong? It's not as if we're dating—though, frankly, it would be none of your business if we were."

Bryan snorted. "Yeah, that's what she said, too."

"Well, then, what's the problem?"

"I don't like it, that's the problem," Bryan said, regarding him defiantly. "Therapy's one thing. This— whatever *this* is—is something else entirely. Kelly's no match for you. She's been in Boston her whole life. She's dated some, but the men were nothing like you."

"Which makes her what? Naive? Stupid?"

Bryan's scowl deepened. "Of course not."

"Glad to know you're smart enough to see that. But if Kelly's not the problem, then I must be," Michael concluded. "Do you figure I'm some sort of macho, sex-starved male who can't keep his hormones in check?"

His friend flushed a dull red. "No, but you are experienced."

Michael couldn't deny that. "Maybe so, but I would never take advantage of your sister," he said flatly. "After all the time we spent together, you ought to know me better than that."

"I suppose, but it's been a lot of years since you and I hung out, Michael. You could have changed," Bryan said defensively.

"I haven't," Michael said, meeting his gaze evenly.

Bryan nodded slowly. "I'll take your word, then, that you won't take advantage of her."

"Thank you." He slanted a look at Bryan. "So, does she have any idea you're over here warning me off?"

"Probably," Bryan said.

Michael regarded him with amusement. "And you got out of the house in one piece? Amazing. You must be quicker than I remembered."

"Very funny."

"Look, I admire the fact that you care about what happens to your sister, but I swear to you that I'm not a threat. I'll say it one more time—this whole pub visit is strictly professional. She thinks it will help the therapy if I can put my trust in her."

Bryan rolled his eyes. "And you bought that hogwash?"

Something in his reaction sent a little chill of apprehension down Michael's back. He regarded Bryan with a narrowed gaze. "You think she has another agenda?"

"She might not even be aware of it herself, but, yes, I think she has another agenda." He leveled a warning look at Michael. "And so help me, if you take her up on it and break her heart, I'll make you regret it."

"Whoa!" Michael protested, reeling from the possibility that Bryan viewed his own sister as the one who couldn't be entirely trusted to exercise good judgment. "It's a long way from spending one evening in a pub with family to breaking your sister's heart. Trust me, that is not a road I intend to go down.''

"As long as you're clear on the consequences,'' Bryan said flatly.

"Very clear. Are you clear on the fact that I'm not the least bit interested in getting involved with *anyone* these days? Fixing my own life is pretty much an all-consuming task.''

"Okay, then,'' Bryan said, clearly relieved. "Now turn the sound up on the game, while I get us another beer.''

Michael stared after him as he left the room. Bryan's little wake-up call hadn't exactly scared him. He could handle an irate Bryan. But the memory of the way he'd felt when Kelly had her hands all over him gave him pause. He was suddenly far less confident about whether he could handle Kelly, if she really did have something other than therapy on her mind.

Michael was still feeling a little leery about Kelly's intentions when they got to Ryan's Place on Friday night. Fortunately, with nearly a dozen members of his own family and the O'Briens around, it was easy enough to put some distance between himself and Kelly.

When the boisterous crowd got to be too much for him, he made his way to the bar where Ryan was trying to keep up with the orders. Michael couldn't hide his grin at how natural his big brother looked pouring ales and Irish whisky and joking with the customers.

"This place suits you,'' he told Ryan, when his brother finally turned his attention to him.

"You like it, then?" Ryan asked.

"There's a warm, comfortable feel to it I haven't run across since a vacation in Ireland a few years back."

"Then I've done it right," Ryan said, obviously pleased. "And having you and Sean in here couldn't make me happier. For a long time, I thought I could be content just to have this place with its crowd of regulars. Then Maggie came along and made me see what I was missing." He nodded toward the crowd across the room. "The O'Briens are special. I didn't trust all that love they shower on everyone at first, but it's the real thing."

Michael nodded. "I can see that. Not five seconds after we met, Nell O'Brien fussed over me as if I were one of her own brood."

"You are now," Ryan said simply. His expression turned thoughtful. "You know, if you wanted to invite your foster family here sometime, it would be fine with me. I'd like to get to know them. I never stayed with any of mine long enough to get attached. Sean had better luck, but he doesn't see them much anymore. Of all of us, I think you're the one who came closest to finding a real home."

Michael tried to imagine the Havilceks here and, surprisingly, found that he could. "Maybe I will," he said. "One of these days. I haven't told them I'm back in Boston."

Ryan regarded him with shock. "Why not?"

Michael tried out the same explanation he'd used on Kelly to see if it sounded any better now. "I wanted to sort things out for myself. My foster mom is great, but she'd take over and try to fix things." He grinned. "The girls are no better. I had measles when I was maybe eight or nine and they just about nursed me into a mental institution with all their hovering. I couldn't think straight. Even a cold was enough to bring out all their Florence Nightingale tendencies.'' He tapped his still-useless leg. ''Just imagine the frenzy they'd go into over this.''

''Would that be so awful?'' Ryan asked, an unmistakable trace of envy in his voice.

Michael sighed. He'd learned only a little of what his big brother had gone through in foster care, but he knew their experiences were vastly different. He could understand why Ryan might not get how Michael would chafe under all that attention. ''Trust me, it's better this way. They'd be hurt if I refused to move in with one of them.''

''Will they be any less hurt when they find out you've been hiding out from them for months?''

''Not months,'' Michael insisted. ''Another week or two, just till I see if my prognosis improves at all.''

Ryan nodded. ''Okay, then, I'll back off for now.'' He glanced across the room. ''I was a little surprised to see Kelly and her brother with you tonight.''

Michael shook his head, thinking about how complicated this simple outing had turned out to be. ''Kelly's here because she thinks therapy will go more smoothly if I start to trust her.''

''And Bryan?''

''He's here because he's afraid I'm going to make a move on Kelly,'' Michael admitted dryly.

Ryan barely contained a chuckle. ''And do you intend to make a move on her? You could do a lot worse, you know.''

Michael turned and studied Kelly. She was a beautiful woman, no question about it. And there were definitely some sparks between them. Even so, he shook his head. "Too complicated."

"Because you and Bryan are friends?"

"No, because she's my best shot at getting out of this wheelchair. I don't intend to do anything that might distract from that."

Ryan's gaze narrowed. "There are a lot of therapists in Boston, you know. Maggie's still got her copy of that list she made. A new therapist could uncomplicate things."

"I've made my peace with having Kelly underfoot. I don't want to start over," Michael said flatly.

"That might be a shortsighted view, especially if you're attracted to her," Ryan said, refusing to let the subject drop.

"I'm not," Michael insisted.

A grin spread across Ryan's face. "I hope you were more convincing when you tried that line out on her brother."

Michael sighed. "Probably not."

"Just make me a promise, then," Ryan pleaded. "When you two decide to have it out, don't do it in here, okay? The bar glass is expensive."

"I'll keep that in mind." Michael glanced toward Kelly and saw that she was watching him. "Guess I'd better bite the bullet and get back over there. I've managed to stay out of Kelly's path most of the evening, which pretty much defeats the avowed purpose of bringing her here."

Ryan stepped out from behind the bar and blocked his path. "Look, I know you didn't ask for any advice from your big brother, but I'm going to offer some just the same. Therapy might get you back on your feet, but it's going to take more than that to heal your soul. If Kelly's offering more, don't be so quick to turn your back on it.''

"I suppose you gave in the very first second that Maggie came into your life," Michael speculated.

Ryan laughed. "Hardly. I'm just trying to save you a little time. You can learn from my mistakes and give in to the inevitable.''

"There's nothing inevitable about Kelly and me."

"If you say so," Ryan said doubtfully.

"I do," Michael said very firmly.

Unfortunately, Ryan didn't look as if he believed the denial any more than Michael did himself.

In terms of building a bridge between herself and Michael, the evening had been a bust so far, Kelly concluded as he rejoined the group who'd clustered around several tables in the middle of the pub. She noted he was careful to stay on the opposite side of the table from her.

Unfortunately for him, Bryan had just asked Katie O'Brien to dance, so the chair right next to Michael had just opened up. She made her way around the table.

"You've been avoiding me," she accused lightly as she took the vacant seat.

"Bryan's orders," he said just as lightly.

She laughed. "I probably ought to kill him."

"You probably should."

"Then, again, I'm surprised you scared off so easily."

"A smart man knows to pick his battles and his enemies."

Kelly regarded him with dismay. "Is that what I am, the enemy?''

He winced. "No, of course not. Neither is your brother. We're just caught up in a complicated situation."

"It doesn't have to be all that complicated. I'm trying to get to know you. I'm not asking you to marry me or even to sleep with me."

"Thank heavens for that," he said fervently. "Your brother really would kill me, then."

She decided to play it cool. "Only if you took me up on it," she teased. "Would you?"

"Kelly." Her name came out part warning, part plea.

"Yes?"

"You're playing a dangerous game."

"Only if you're the least bit tempted," she said.

"I'm a man," he said, as if that said it all.

"So, of course, you're not capable of resisting temptation?" she scoffed. "Please, Michael. Don't try to make me believe you'd take advantage of the situation, if I happened to throw myself at you."

A dull flush crept into his cheeks. "We're never going to know, because you are not going to do that. Are we clear?"

The direct order made her see red. Something dark and dangerous came to life inside her. Before he could make his demand again, she leaned forward, clamped a hand around the back of his neck and kissed him.

Somewhere in the back of her mind, she'd only intended the gesture to be a belligerent response to his unreasonable order. Big mistake. No, *huge* mistake. Because the instant her lips met the hard line of his mouth, she felt as if the entire world was spinning out of control.

And when his mouth opened and his tongue thrust

between her lips, she was completely lost to sensation…greedy, urgent sensation that made her pulse hum and her heart thump wildly. Liquid heat pooled low in her belly and desire made her want to cling and savor and taste. Only a low growl in Michael's throat had her tearing herself away, her cheeks flushed, her breath coming in quick, unsteady gasps.

She rocked back in her chair and raked her fingers through her hair. "I'm sorry," she whispered, embarrassment flooding through her. Only the dazed look in Michael's eyes kept her from feeling like a complete fool.

"Don't," he said, his voice harsh. "Don't apologize. I shouldn't have—"

She cut him off. "Shouldn't have what?" she asked with self-derision. "Responded when I all but attacked you?"

He smiled faintly at that. "I dared you," he pointed out.

"You did not," she said, then thought about it. Maybe he hadn't dared her in so many words, but the challenge in his voice was exactly what she'd responded to. She studied him in confusion. "Okay, maybe you did. Did you do it on purpose?"

He looked almost as bewildered as she felt. "I wish to hell I knew."

Before they could explore it any further, her brother arrived, a glowering expression on his face. "I see that my warning was taken to heart by both of you."

"Oh, stuff a sock in it," Kelly retorted.

Bryan ignored her and looked at Michael. "What about you?" he demanded indignantly. "What do you have to say for yourself?"

"I think 'stuff a sock in it' pretty well sums up my view, as well."

Bryan scowled from Michael to Kelly and back again. "Okay, then, I wash my hands of this. You two are on your own."

"Fine by me," Kelly retorted.

"I always have been," Michael said, his expression already distant and withdrawn.

Bryan hesitated. He seemed as if he were about to relent, but then he whirled around and headed for the bar.

Kelly instinctively reached for Michael's hands and held them tightly. "You are not on your own anymore. Look around you. You never have to be alone again."

Michael surveyed the assembled Devaneys and O'Briens warily, as if he still didn't quite trust what they were offering. In that instant, Kelly felt something deep inside herself shift. Years ago what she had felt for Michael Devaney had been a teenage crush on a handsome, mysterious boy. What she felt right now was so much more. She wasn't quite ready to put a label on it, especially not one he would reject out of hand.

But if it took her a lifetime, she would find some way to wipe that bleak expression from his eyes and prove to him that he was a man worthy of being loved.

Chapter Five

The memory of that soul-searing kiss kept Michael awake most of the night. It had taken him totally by surprise on so many levels, his mind was still reeling.

Even after Bryan's warning, he hadn't actually expected Kelly to make a move on him. A part of him still thought of her as Bryan's kid sister. That she had impulsively and thoroughly out-of-the-blue locked lips with him had shocked him right down to his toes. That wasn't some kid's move. It was the act of a woman willing to take what she wanted.

That he had responded, that he had all but devoured her right there in the middle of his brother's pub in front of a whole slew of witnesses—including her disapproving brother—had been almost as shocking. Maybe that head injury he'd dismissed had left his brain more addled than he'd realized.

He'd admitted to Kelly that part of the blame was

his. He had—albeit unintentionally—pretty much challenged her to kiss him. What red-blooded, healthy, spirited woman wouldn't have reacted exactly as Kelly had? That didn't make it right. It certainly didn't make it smart. And it most definitely didn't make it something that could be allowed to happen again.

Unfortunately, short of firing her, he wasn't entirely clear on how he was going to guarantee that there wouldn't be a repeat, especially now that they both knew exactly the kind of fireworks they'd be avoiding. Most men—and even a few women—would not willingly turn their backs on that kind of instantaneous combustion, no matter how dangerous.

Michael muttered a sharp oath under his breath. Why hadn't he seen that kiss coming? He could have deflected it, laughed off the incident and gotten a decent night's sleep. Instead, he'd tossed and turned, his body half-aroused by lingering memories of the way Kelly's mouth had felt on his. Here it was nearly eight in the morning and he was as stirred up as he had been within seconds after she'd dragged her lips away from his. Worst of all, there wasn't even enough time for him to haul himself into an ice-cold shower before Kelly arrived for their Saturday morning session.

Well, there was only one thing to do, he finally concluded. He had to face the whole situation squarely and give Kelly the option of quitting or sticking around under a stringent set of hands-off guidelines.

There was just one tiny little flaw in that plan. Massages were part of the therapy. He'd discovered already that there were a dozen different reasons why it was necessary for her to touch him. Trying to ban all contact between them was pretty much self-defeating in terms of his recovery. Not banning it was dangerous for entirely different reasons.

Michael thought of the thousand and one dangerous situations in which he'd found himself during his years as a SEAL. How could he possibly let one sexy little therapist scare him out of doing what needed to be done? He couldn't, not if he ever expected to look at himself in the mirror again.

Bring her on, he thought with renewed determination. Let her tempt him. He would be strong. He would resist. He would concentrate on the reason she was in his life...to make him whole again, to get him back on his feet. He would pretend she looked like a frog and had the skin of an alligator.

He choked on the image. Maybe he should forget about trying to deceive himself into thinking she wasn't attractive and concentrate on developing the willpower of a saint.

"You did what?" Kelly's boss at the rehab clinic asked incredulously when Kelly stopped by with coffee and blueberry muffins on her way to Michael's on Saturday morning.

The coffee and treats were a Saturday ritual. The stunned expression on Moira's face was a rarity. So was the hard look that followed. Kelly found herself wincing under that intense, disapproving scrutiny.

"Tell me again," Moira commanded. "I can't believe I heard you right the first time."

"I kissed Michael," Kelly repeated. "I flat out, on the lips, kissed him." Her chin shot up in a display of defiance. "And I would do it again, if I got the chance."

That said, her belligerence wilted. "Not that I'm ever likely to have another chance," she said. "He'll probably fire me when I walk in there this morning."

"He should," Moira said without the slightest trace of sympathy. "Of all the unprofessional, self-defeating things you could have done—"

Kelly cut her off. The lecture wasn't really unexpected, but it was unnecessary. "You're not telling me anything I haven't already told myself a thousand times since last night. What do I do now?"

"Go over there and face the music," Moira said. "And don't be surprised if it's a funeral dirge."

"That's what I love about you, Moira. You always paint such a rosy picture of things," Kelly said wryly.

"What did you expect?"

"I suppose I was hoping you'd mix a tiny bit of compassion in with the lecture," she admitted. "Imagine that this was a guy you'd had the hots for during most of your adult life. Wouldn't you have done exactly what I did, given the chance?"

"You weren't exactly given the chance," Moira reminded her. "You stole it."

"A technicality," Kelly insisted. "Remember, he did kiss me back."

"Which only proves he's a red-blooded male."

"You don't intend to give an inch on this, do you?" Kelly asked wearily.

"And let you off the hook? No way." Moira's disapproving frown did lift ever so slightly, though. She leaned forward and subjected Kelly to a thorough survey. "Judging from the pink in your cheeks and the sparkle in your eyes, the kiss must have been worth putting your professional reputation on the line."

Kelly sighed. "Oh, yes," she confided dreamily.

"That kiss was everything I ever dreamed of, and then some. I can only imagine what kissing him would be like if his heart was really in it."

"Probably best not to go there," Moira said. "You might be tempted to try it again."

"Oh, I suspect I will be," Kelly admitted. Before her friend could react to that, she squared her shoulders with renewed resolve. "But the next time, I'm going to resist. I'm going to remind myself that I am not in Michael's life as a woman, but as a therapist. That I have a job to do, and I won't be able to do it if there's all that kissing going on."

"Great logic," Moira said, laughing. "Tell me again why you were at the pub."

"So we could get to know each other better."

"Well, kissing would definitely accomplish that," Moira noted.

"Actually, it was all about gaining his trust," Kelly corrected. "I don't think the kissing accomplished that. If anything, it probably did the exact opposite. He's probably terrified to be alone in a room with me for fear I'll find some new way to test his code of honor."

"Could be," Moira confirmed. "I guess you'll find that out when you get over there."

Kelly sighed. "And there's no point in putting that off, is there? Wish me luck."

"Always," her friend said, her expression sobering. "I just wish I knew if you wanted luck on the professional front or the personal."

"That is the heart of the dilemma, isn't it?" Kelly said as she left Moira's office to make the drive to Michael's.

Until she heard him call out in response to her ringing of the bell, she wasn't sure she would even find him at home. Apparently he was less cowardly about this meeting than she was. She wanted to turn and run.

She didn't, though. She walked into the apartment with her head held high and a plan forming in the back of her mind for keeping Michael as a client despite her behavior the night before. One look at him had all of that flying right out of her mind.

"What happened? Are you sick?" she demanded, taking in his ashen complexion, unshaved cheeks and still-mussed hair.

"No sleep," he said tersely. "I finally gave up about twenty minutes ago. I haven't even had my first cup of coffee."

Her heart skipped a heat. "Why were you having trouble sleeping?"

"Do you even need to ask?" he asked, his expression daunting.

Kelly winced at his harsh tone. "The unfortunate kiss," she said.

"The unfortunate, never-to-be-repeated kiss," he confirmed, then almost immediately scowled at her. "There you go again."

She stared at him in confusion. "What?"

"What I said before, it was not a challenge."

"Of course not," Kelly agreed at once, though she had to admit a tiny part of her had reared up in defiance of that *never-to-be-repeated* edict.

"Then why did you get that same glint in your eyes that you got last night right before you kissed the daylights out of me?" he asked.

Kelly stared at him. "A glint? Really?"

"Don't give me that innocent look. If I'm going to

have to watch every word out of my mouth around you, this is never going to work. I can't have you thinking that everything I say is some sort of challenge or invitation or something.''

Kelly seized on the fact that he apparently hadn't decided to fire her outright. "I'll behave myself. I promise. What happened last night was a fluke. I swear to you that I am not in the habit of throwing myself at my clients."

"Good to know," he said, his mood lightening ever so slightly. "How did you happen to make an exception in my case?"

"Like I said, it was a fluke. I must have had too much to drink."

"One ale that you nursed all night?" he asked skeptically.

Kelly shrugged. "I'm not a big drinker."

A grin tugged at his lips. "Also very good to know. I guess it wouldn't be wise to invite you over for beers and basketball."

"I don't think the basketball would be a problem," she said thoughtfully, then winced as his grin spread. "Sorry. You were teasing."

"Just a little," he conceded.

"Michael, I really am sorry. What I did was inappropriate and unprofessional, and I assure you that it won't happen again. I hope you'll give me another chance." She drew in a deep breath, then dove into her planned speech. "In fact, I was thinking that we could move the sessions to the rehab center where I work part-time, if that would make you feel more comfortable. There would be other patients, other therapists around. We'd never be alone." She'd figured that alone would sell him on the idea, but just in case it wasn't enough, she added, "And there is equipment there that would be helpful."

His frown deepened as she spoke. "Forget the center. I don't want to work with a lot of people staring at me. We can go on working right here."

"But the equipment there really would be helpful. At some point you'll need to go there, anyway."

"When that time comes, we'll discuss it," he said flatly, clearly refusing to give the idea any more consideration. "Not until then. As for avoiding a repeat of what happened last night, I told you then that part of the blame is mine. I take full responsibility for my part in it, and you've apologized for yours. That's sufficient. We'll just forget about this and make sure it never happens again. There's no point in denying that there's some sort of attraction going on here, but we're both adults. We can deal with it and keep ourselves from acting on it." He met her gaze. "Deal?"

"Deal," she agreed eagerly, so overcome with relief that she wanted to hug him, but wisely managed to resist. Instead, she injected a brisk note in her voice and said, "Now, why don't I make some coffee and we can get started?"

"The coffee can wait," Michael said. "We've already wasted too much of this session. I want you to give me a real workout today, and in case there's any doubt in your mind, that *is* a challenge, and I expect you to take me up on it."

Kelly nodded. She didn't even try to hide her relief that he was giving her a second chance. And if the only thing he wanted from her was a grueling schedule of therapy, she would bury the memory of just how good that kiss had been and accommodate him.

At least for now.

* * *

The increasingly demanding exercises were excruciatingly painful. Sweat was beading on Michael's brow, but Kelly had asked for ten more repetitions and, by God, he was going to give her ten. A SEAL never quit. Sometimes, in the weeks and months following his injury, he'd had a hard time remembering that. For a few weeks in San Diego, the news had been relentlessly discouraging. Eventually he'd taken it to heart and resigned himself to his sedentary fate.

But ever since the morning after that unforgettable kiss, Kelly had flatly refused to let him sink for one single second into a morass of self-pity. Whenever he muttered about all this effort being a waste of time, she sent him a chiding look and demanded even more from him. In the last couple of weeks, he'd learned to keep his mouth shut and do whatever she asked without protest.

The two hours she spent with him three days a week flew by. And after she left, it took him hours to recover from pushing himself to the limit, but he would not allow himself to quit.

She thought he was making excellent progress. He disagreed, but kept his opinion to himself. If he so much as hinted that he was discouraged, he was afraid that one of these days she would stop responding with extra work and simply walk out the door. If she did that, she would take his only hope with her.

Besides, aside from the rigors of her therapy, he enjoyed spending time with her. He liked the way she got in his face, refusing to back down. He liked even more the faint feminine scent she wore. He was beginning to remember just how much he liked having a woman in his life. Not one special woman, just someone to flirt with, maybe dance with, make love to.

He sighed, then realized that Kelly was staring at him with a puzzled expression.

"Where did you go just then?" she asked. "You stopped right in the middle of the eighth leg lift."

"Sorry. I guess my mind wandered."

"Really?"

"It happens," he said gruffly.

"Of course it does, but you're usually so focused."

He reached for a towel and wiped his face. "Well, today I'm not. Sue me."

There was no mistaking the hurt in Kelly's eyes. It wrenched Michael's heart. He honestly couldn't blame her for being on the brink of tears. His mind had wandered down a forbidden path and now he was unreasonably taking it out on her. Why was it that he could look into the eyes of soulless terrorists and remain completely unmoved, but one glance into Kelly's soft gray eyes and he was lost?

"Sorry," he said, apologizing yet again for his thoughtless behavior.

"Why don't we quit for the day?" she suggested, her tone neutral. "You've been working too hard for the past couple of weeks. You could use a break."

Michael was smart enough to acknowledge that she was right. He had been overexerting himself and his muscles were complaining. The last thing he needed was a tear or some other injury that would put his rehabilitation on hold. Nor did he need to risk offending Kelly any more than he had already.

"I'll tell you what," he said, trying to make amends. "I need to go see someone today. If you have time to give me a lift over there, I'll buy you lunch on the way.''

Kelly seemed so taken aback by the suggestion, he couldn't help chuckling. ''I'm not scared to be alone in a car with you,'' he teased. ''Or in a restaurant. You've been on very good behavior lately. I think I can let down my guard for a couple of hours.''

She gave him a rueful smile. ''You have no idea how stressful it's been,'' she responded.

Michael had the distinct impression that she wasn't actually joking. He could understand exactly where she was coming from. Despite his overwhelming relief that they'd been adhering to the ground rules about no intimate contact, the strain of it was telling on him, too. Maybe that was one more reason why he'd suggested lunch. He figured they both deserved a reward for their incredible restraint.

''Probably best not to go down that road,'' he told her. ''Not when we've been doing so well.''

An expression of what might have been disappointment flashed in her eyes, but then she regained her composure.

''So where are you going that you're willing to risk spending time alone in a car with me? It must be important.''

He nodded slowly. ''It is. I'm going to stop by to see the Havilceks.''

''Your family,'' she said at once, her expression brightening. ''I met your mother a few times when we were kids. I guess she was actually your foster mother, though, right?''

He nodded. ''I didn't think of her that way, not for long, anyway. She wouldn't allow it. She said that even if she couldn't adopt me, she intended to be my mother. No boy could have had a better one.''

''Then why have you waited so long to get in touch with her since you got back to Boston?'' she asked. ''I still don't understand that.''

''Self-protection,'' he admitted candidly. ''She's the kind of woman who assesses a situation, then takes over. It doesn't matter to her that I've been a grown man for a long time and that I've handled extraordinary responsibilities with the Navy, I'm still her baby.''

''Hard to picture anyone thinking of you that way,'' Kelly said, surveying him with blatant appreciation. ''Then again, that's exactly how my folks treat Bryan and me. It would probably help if Bryan and I moved into our own places, but it's been so comfortable living at home, neither of us have bothered. Hovering and worrying is probably just a universal parental trait.''

''That doesn't make it any less annoying, especially in a situation like this,'' Michael said.

''No, it certainly doesn't.'' Kelly regarded him with undisguised curiosity. ''Do you remember your real…'' She immediately stopped and corrected herself, ''I mean, your biological mother at all?''

Michael had thought about that very question a lot over the years, even more so since Ryan and Sean had found him in San Diego. They both had such vivid memories of their mother, but Michael's were all hazy. When Mother's Day rolled around, it was Doris Havilcek—with her sweet smile, graying hair, sharp intelligence and steely resolve—whose image filled his head. Kathleen Devaney was a name on his birth certificate, nothing more. She stirred no sentimental feelings in him at all.

"Not really," he told Kelly. "I don't have the same kind of anger about her and my dad that Ryan and Sean feel, either. Maybe if I'd been a little older or if I'd wound up in a different situation the way they did, I'd hate them, too, but basically when it comes to my biological parents, I feel nothing at all."

Sorrow spread across Kelly's expressive face. "Aren't you even the least bit curious about them? I know I would be. I'd want to know what they're like, why they did what they did, where they are now."

"Why bother?" he said cynically. "There are no good explanations for any of it. If it were up to me, Ryan would give up searching for them, but he's determined to finish what he started. Sean has some reservations, but in general, I think he's backing him up. I think one reason they're so determined to find our parents is to find out what happened to the twins. For all we know, they were abandoned along the way, too, when it got to be too inconvenient to keep them around."

"Twins?" Kelly repeated incredulously. "There were more of you?"

He nodded. "Twin brothers, Patrick and Daniel. They were only two when we were all split up. Ryan seems convinced our parents took them when they left." He tried to dismiss the little twinge of dismay that stirred in him, but he wasn't entirely successful. If it was true, it made the whole mess even more despicable.

He met Kelly's gaze. "If you ask me, Ryan's going to be opening up a whole lot of emotional garbage by tracking them down. If they did have all those years with our parents, how the hell are they supposed to react when three older brothers come charging back into their lives? And I doubt if either Ryan or Sean can claim to be entirely indifferent to the fact that our parents chose to keep Patrick and Daniel while dumping the rest of us into foster care.''

''But it could be wonderful to be reunited,'' Kelly insisted.

''Maybe in an ideal world,'' Michael said. ''But something tells me it's not going to be a picture-perfect moment, not for anyone.''

He shrugged off his dread of that day and forced a smile. ''Have you actually agreed to my invitation yet?''

She laughed. ''Probably not, but if you think I'd miss the chance to see you reunited with your mom, you're crazy. Of course I'll take you, and lunch will be great.''

''You won't mind pushing me around in this chair?'' he asked, even though the real question was how he was going to feel letting her do it. He had a hunch she'd be more comfortable in the situation than he was likely to be.

''Don't be ridiculous,'' she said, confirming his guess. ''But you might want to change first. Otherwise the restaurant's likely to make us eat outside, even though the temperature's in the teens today.''

Michael glanced at his sweaty workout clothes and feigned indignation. ''You think I need to improve on this?''

''Oh, yeah,'' she said fervently. ''Not that I haven't always been rather fond of a truly male scent, but everyone's not like me.''

"Maybe you should come back in a half hour," he suggested.

She frowned at him. "Make it an hour. I could use a little sprucing up myself. Will that still give us enough time for lunch before you're due at the Havilceks'?"

"Sure," he said, unwilling to admit that he hadn't exactly warned them that he was coming by. He hadn't wanted to give his mother time to work up a good head of steam about his failure to get in touch the second he hit town. He was hoping the surprise of finding him on her doorstep would take the edge off of her annoyance.

Kelly grinned at him. "You haven't told them you're coming, have you?"

"Nope," he said unrepentantly.

She laughed. "This is going to be fun. I'm not sure which I'm looking forward to more—the joyful reunion or listening to your mother deliver a blistering lecture about the way you've been hiding out in Boston the last few months."

Michael regarded her with chagrin. "Something tells me you'll get a chance to evaluate both options and decide which has the most entertainment value. The only person I've ever met who's tougher on me than you is my mother. None of my commanding officers in the navy even came close."

"Then I can definitely hardly wait to meet her," Kelly said. "Maybe she'll give me some tips on how to handle you."

He leveled a look straight into eyes suddenly churning with emotion. "Trust me, that is not a lesson you need to learn."

Kelly looked incredibly pleased by the backhanded

compliment. "Even an expert can use an occasional pointer from someone with more experience."

Michael groaned. What had he been thinking? The prospect of having Kelly and his mother ganging up on him was almost more daunting than trying to get out of this damned wheelchair.

Chapter Six

Kelly deliberately chose the most wheelchair accessible restaurant she knew for their lunch. Though she wasn't absolutely certain, she was fairly sure that this was the first time Michael had ventured out to eat anyplace other than his brother's pub. She didn't want the experience to be so stressful that he refused to try it again. He was a proud man and he was already chafing enough at letting her assist him with getting in and out of her car.

"Is this okay?" she asked as she walked along beside him as he rolled himself toward the street-level entrance.

"Looks fine," he said, his expression grim as he contemplated the door. When Kelly started toward it, he grabbed her wrist. "I'll get the damn door."

Arguing seemed pointless. She waited until he'd maneuvered himself around and could hold it while she stepped inside. Then he faced the dilemma of how to get in himself without having the door crash into him. His face was a study in concentration as he shouldered the door open, then eased his chair through the entry. She didn't release her pent-up breath until he was safely inside the restaurant.

There were more obstacles to come. The only vacant table in the busy restaurant was all the way across the room. When the room was empty, Kelly imagined the aisles were wide enough, but now with chairs jutting erratically out, they were all but impassable. Michael's expression was filled with tension as he tried to make his way between tables without knocking into the backs of other customers, most of whom were completely oblivious to his difficulties. The hostess had long since placed their menus on the table and gone back to her post by the time Michael finally crossed the room.

"You did great," Kelly said, taking her seat.

"I don't need a pat on the head for getting across a damned restaurant," he snapped.

She bit back a sharp retort of her own and turned her attention to the menu. She was still fighting the sting of tears when she felt his hand cover hers.

"Kelly?"

"What?" she responded, still holding her menu up to mask the fact that she was about to cry over something so ridiculous, especially when she could totally understand his level of exasperation. For a man whose work had required a peak level of physical fitness and agility, to adjust to being anything less had to be difficult.

"I seem to spend my life apologizing to you, but I

am sorry. It's just so damned frustrating to be tied to this chair," Michael said, his tone full of contrition.

She lifted her gaze then and met his. "It won't be forever. And even if it were, it wouldn't be the end of the world."

"It's already the end of my world," he said quietly. "No matter what, I won't be going back to work as a SEAL. For months, in the back of my mind, I was convinced I could if I just worked hard enough." He sighed. "But for weeks now I've been struggling to face the fact that that's not going to happen."

"I know I can't begin to understand what it's like to lose something that's been so important to you, but you will find something else just as challenging," she told him earnestly. "There are plenty of things a man with your intelligence can do. And a career's not everything. You can marry, have a family. Your life isn't over."

"The only one I ever wanted is over," he said flatly.

"If that's going to be your attitude, then I feel sorry for you," she told him, refusing to back down when a dull, red flush climbed into his cheeks. "There are plenty of people who will never walk again. You *will* get out of that wheelchair. So it's taking a little longer than you'd like. And you won't be able to do some of the rigorous things you once did, so what? You're alive, dammit! Stop feeling so sorry for yourself and concentrate on what you still have, instead of what you've lost."

For what seemed like an eternity she wasn't sure if he was going to explode with anger or simply turn around and wheel himself right back out of the restaurant. She was still wondering when their waiter appeared and, completely oblivious to the tension, announced that he was Henry and he'd be taking care of them today.

"Just what I need," Michael muttered. "Somebody else who thinks it's his mission in life to take care of me."

Henry stared at him in confusion. "What? Did I say something wrong?"

Michael's smile wasn't exactly wholehearted, but it was a smile. "No, I'm just having a bad day. How's your day going, Henry?"

Henry still looked uncertain, but he said gamely, "Fine, sir. Have you two decided on what you'd like to drink?"

Michael glanced questioningly toward Kelly.

"I'll have a cup of tea," she said.

Michael nodded. "The lady will have tea, and I'll have your strongest poison."

Henry blinked furiously. "Sir?"

Kelly bit back a chuckle. "Don't mind him, Henry. He thinks he's being amusing. Bring him a cup of very strong coffee. I want him wide-awake while I finish telling him what I think of him."

"Yes, ma'am," the waiter said, backing away from the table with undisguised relief.

"Think he'll ever come back?" Michael asked.

"He shouldn't," Kelly said. "You were awful to him."

"And to you," Michael said. "I thought I'd save you the trouble of having to put something lethal in my coffee by asking him to do it."

"Don't think I wouldn't, if I had any murderous tendencies," Kelly told him. "Unfortunately, I still think you're worth salvaging."

He studied her intently. "Why?"

"Why what?"

"Why do you think I'm worth saving?"

She got the impression that he sincerely wanted to know, maybe even needed to know. "Because underneath all that exasperating self-pity, you're a good guy. You've spent your life being a hero for your country. You're smart, occasionally funny and breathtakingly handsome, though I wouldn't let that go to your head. Good looks rarely make up for a lousy disposition."

A smile tugged at his lips. "I'll try to remember that from now on."

Kelly regarded him seriously. "Michael, there really are a lot of blessings in your life. You should try counting them, instead of focusing on what you've lost."

"I will," he promised, his own expression suddenly serious. "I hope you won't mind if I put you at the top of the list."

Kelly's breath caught in her throat and the tears she'd fought off returned with a vengeance. "Dammit, why did you have to go and say something so blasted sweet?" she asked, swiping impatiently at her cheeks. "I was just getting comfortable being furious with you."

He reached over and caught a tear streaking down her face, then brushed it gently away. "Well, now, I couldn't have that, could I?"

She sniffed and tried not to notice the way his fingers felt against her skin. "Why not?"

"You were liable to go off and leave me stranded in here," he told her with a perfectly straight face.

Kelly choked back the laughter that bubbled up. "I

should have known your reason would be totally self-serving."

He grinned. "That's the kind of guy I am," he said unrepentantly.

"No," she said emphatically. "That's the kind of guy you want me to *think* you are." She leveled a look deep into his eyes. "Which makes me wonder why you feel it's necessary. Are you deliberately trying to scare me off, Michael? Is this part of your tactic to keep some distance between us?"

He seemed to consider the question for an eternity before finally shrugging. "I honestly don't know."

"Then you should know that it takes a lot more than a bad temper to scare me away."

He sighed heavily. "Yeah, I think I'd already figured that out."

The entire scene at the restaurant had been totally draining. Given a choice, Michael would have gone back to his own apartment and hidden out for the rest of the day, but he wasn't about to admit to Kelly just how shaken he was, both by the struggles he'd had adjusting to a world in which he wasn't agile as a cat and to the discovery that her opinion of him mattered. It mattered far more than it should.

Which was also why he wasn't going to back out on this visit to see his folks. He wasn't going to give Kelly one more reason to think of him as a coward.

Given his state of emotional turmoil, he shouldn't have been surprised by his reaction to seeing the home in which he'd grown up, but he was. It was as if a hard knot he hadn't even known was there, deep inside, finally eased.

The house, an unimpressive, two-story brick Co-

lonial on a quiet street, looked exactly the way it had
since the first day he'd walked through the door.
There was ivy climbing up one side, despite his father's frequent attempts to destroy it. The shutters,
despite his mother's avowed intention to paint them
red, were still the glossy black his father preferred, as
was the front door with its gleaming brass knocker.
His gaze drifted along the front walk, then froze at
the sight of the steps. There were so blasted many of
them. How had he forgotten?

Apparently Kelly saw his dilemma at the same instant, but she was quicker to adjust. ''You can go in
through the garage,'' she said swiftly. ''It opens directly into the kitchen, doesn't it?''

Michael didn't bother asking how she knew that.
She had been in the house from time to time. If the
visits hadn't been especially memorable to him, apparently they had been to her. He was grateful for that
at the moment.

''That'll work,'' he said at once. ''The garage
door's not locked and it's not automatic. Think you
can lift it?''

She grinned and feigned flexing a muscle. ''I may
be little, but I'm mighty.''

She went on ahead as Michael tried to navigate the
driveway. It seemed to take forever. He was surprised
that no one glanced outside and caught a glimpse of
him struggling up the slight incline. What if no one
was home? Granted it was Saturday afternoon and his
mother had always baked on Saturdays, but maybe
things had changed.

As he considered that, he realized that Kelly had
the garage door open. His mother's car, the same dull
gray sedan she'd driven for far too many years now,

was right where it had always been. He bit back a sigh as he thought of how many times he'd offered her money to buy herself something newer, and how many times she'd told him to save his money for a rainy day.

Just then the door from the kitchen was flung open and there she was, her cheeks rosy from the heat of the oven, wisps of graying curls framing her face and an expression of pure delight on her face.

"Oh, my," his mother whispered. "I heard the garage door, but I never imagined… Oh, my." She was down the driveway, her arms around him before Michael could even blink away the tears that threatened.

"Mom, you have to stop crying," he said as he held her tightly. "I'm okay, and any second now you're going to have me blubbering. How will that look?"

"I don't care how it looks," she said, still not releasing him. She shook him just a little. "There's nothing wrong with a man showing emotion. I thought I'd taught you that."

Michael laughed. "You certainly tried."

His mother stood up at last, then surveyed him thoroughly. "Oh, Michael, you look wonderful. Why didn't you let us know you were coming?"

"I didn't want you to make a fuss," he said, knowing now how futile that had been. Surprise or no surprise, there would eventually be a fuss. He took her hand and gestured toward the garage. "There's someone here you've been ignoring. Do you remember Kelly Andrews?"

His mother spun around, and her eyes lit up. "Bryan's little sister," she said at once, then grinned. "The one who always had a crush on you."

Michael winced. "Mom, don't embarrass her."

But Kelly was laughing. "And I thought I'd hidden it so well."

"A mother always knows," his mother told her. "It's wonderful to see you again. But how...?" Understanding obviously dawned, and she whirled on him. "Michael Devaney, how long have you been back in Boston?"

"Not long," he said evasively.

She turned to Kelly. "How long?"

Kelly looked straight at him and didn't even hesitate. "I believe it's been about six weeks now, hasn't it, Michael?"

"Traitor," he said.

"Honesty should be prized," his mother scolded. "What on earth am I thinking keeping the two of you out here when it's bitter cold? Come inside where it's warm, so I won't feel guilty making you listen to me tell you just how annoyed I am with you, Michael Devaney."

He felt a little like saying, "Aw, Ma, do I have to?" Unfortunately he knew exactly the sort of reaction that would get. He might as well go in and get the deserved lecture over with.

Looking up, he gave his mother his most appealing smile. "I don't suppose you've been baking today, have you?"

She frowned at him, though there was a twinkle in her eyes. "I've just finished baking for the social hour after church tomorrow, as you perfectly well know, since I've been doing it every Saturday for the past thirty or more years. I don't imagine anyone there will object if I cut one of the apple pies for you and

Kelly.'' She gave him a knowing look. ''And I imagine you'll be wanting ice cream on top.''

''Is there any other way?'' he asked as his mother stepped behind the chair and briskly wheeled it inside as if she'd been doing exactly that forever.

The kitchen smelled of cinnamon and sugar and apples. While he and Kelly took off their coats, his mother bustled around cutting the pie, putting ice cream on top and setting it on the table. Only after he'd taken the first bite and made all the appropriate comments about her incredible baking did she pull out a chair and glower at him.

''Now, then,'' she said in a tone with which he was all too familiar, ''we'll talk about why in heaven's name you thought you had to keep your presence here in Boston a secret from me.''

Kelly grinned and settled back more comfortably in her chair. ''I think I'm going to enjoy seeing you try to wriggle off the hook.''

His mother frowned at her. ''You're not off the hook, either, young lady. You know the phone number here. You could have tipped me off.''

Kelly instantly looked so incredibly guilty that Michael took pity on her. ''Don't blame her. I swore her to secrecy.''

It was a slight overstatement of the truth, but Kelly didn't deserve to get one of his mother's blistering lectures on his account. Hiding out had been his choice, though for the life of him, he couldn't think now why he had thought it was necessary.

''Then you explain it,'' his mother challenged.

He met her gaze and said simply, ''I needed to get my bearings.''

"And you couldn't do that under this roof?" she demanded incredulously.

"No," he said quietly. "I'm not the same man I was when I left here."

"Don't be ridiculous," his mother said with obvious impatience. "Of course, you are, certainly in every way that counts. You're going to have to do much better than that, Michael."

Both women seemed to be watching him expectantly, but Michael didn't have any answers for them. None his mother was likely to accept, certainly.

"I'm glad I'm here now, Mom. Isn't that enough?"

Her eyes misted again. "Yes, I suppose it is," she said softly, then reached for his hand. "Your father is going to be so pleased. He'll be home soon. You can wait, can't you? And I can call your sisters. I'm sure they'd want to be here to welcome you."

Michael noticed that even without him having to say it, she'd apparently gotten the message that he wouldn't be staying here with them. "Of course I can wait, as long as Kelly's not in a rush."

She immediately shook her head. "I'm in no rush. In fact, that will give me time to try to pry this pie recipe out of your mother."

Nothing Kelly could have said would have done more to ingratiate her with his mother, Michael thought as he saw the pleasure bloom on Doris Havilcek's face. Before he knew it the two of them were sharing recipes as if they'd been at it for years. He sat back, closed his eyes for an instant and let the sound of their excited talk flow over him.

It didn't take long for the rest of his family to assemble. His foster sisters Jan and Patty, were the first to arrive, welcoming him with hugs and more stern admonishments about his failure to get in touch the instant he hit town. He was trying to fend them off with good-natured teasing when the man he'd always considered his father walked in.

Kenneth Havilcek was a big, burly man who'd spent his life in construction. He'd loved athletics and privately bemoaned the fact that his daughters weren't the least bit interested in any of the sports he loved. When Michael had come into his life, he'd said Michael was the gift of a son he'd been dreaming about. Sports had been their bond. No father could have been prouder when Michael excelled at both football and basketball in high school. He'd never missed a single game.

He was halfway across the room, a welcoming smile on his face, when he spotted the wheelchair and faltered. When he finally met Michael's gaze, there was a shared misery in his expression. Clearly, he understood better than most of the others in the room the full implications of Michael being unable to walk, however temporarily.

The moment lasted only a heartbeat, then he was bending over, giving Michael a hearty bear hug and a slap on the back. "Welcome home, son. I imagine your mother has already given you an earful about keeping us in the dark about being in Boston, so I won't add to it." He waved a finger under Michael's nose. "But don't think for a second I'm not as irritated by it as she is."

"Sorry, sir."

His father nodded. "I should think you would be. Now, then, what's this I've been hearing about your biological brothers finding you?"

His sisters reacted with shock. "You've heard from them?" Jan demanded. "Why didn't anybody tell me?"

"Or me?" Patty asked. "This is huge news. Where are they? Have you actually seen them? What are they like?"

Michael held up his hands. "Whoa! One question at a time. They came to San Diego when I was in the hospital, so, yes, I have seen them."

"*They* were in San Diego and you wouldn't let us come?" Jan said, her indignation plain.

"I didn't invite them," he protested. "They showed up."

"I guess there's a lesson there for us," Patty said to her sister. "When it comes to our baby brother, we shouldn't wait for an invitation. So where do they live? What are they like?"

"They're right here in Boston," he admitted. "We have a lot of old baggage to work out, but I do like them. And they're dying to meet all of you. Ryan would like you to join us at his pub one evening."

Patty stared at him with sudden comprehension. "Not Ryan's Place?"

Michael nodded. "You know it?"

"I've been there half a dozen times for the Irish music. Ryan is your brother? I can't believe it." She tilted her head and studied him. "Now that you say it, though, I can see the resemblance. This is so amazing. When can we go?"

Everything was moving a little too fast for Michael. He wasn't sure what sort of reaction he'd expected from his family, but it hadn't been this. Then, again, he should have known that people who could welcome a little boy into their home with such open hearts would be just as eager to welcome those who mattered to him.

"How about next Friday night?" he said eventually. He turned his gaze to Kelly, who'd been sitting quietly throughout his reunion with his father and sisters. "Can you make it then?"

Michael caught the pleased look that his mother exchanged with his father and knew exactly what it meant. She already had him romantically linked with Kelly, though they'd never given her so much as a hint that Kelly was anything more than his therapist.

Kelly must have seen the same look, because she hesitated.

"I'd like you to come," he told her, not sure why he felt it was so important to include her. He just knew that this whole day had been easier because she was by his side. He wanted her there when his two families met for the first time. "Please."

She smiled then. "Of course, I'll come," she said, studying him intently. "But if you don't mind, I think we should be going now."

His sisters protested, but his mother took Kelly's side and within minutes Michael was outside in Kelly's car. He glanced over at her as they pulled away.

"How did you know I was ready to leave?" he asked.

She shrugged off the intuition. "Something in your eyes, I suppose."

Michael sighed. It should be terrifying that she could read him so easily, but for some reason, it wasn't. Tomorrow, when he was less exhausted, he'd have to try to figure out why.

Chapter Seven

Kelly had known she was in serious emotional trouble the minute she'd started sharing recipes with Doris Havilcek. There had been something so wonderfully comfortable about it, as if she were already a member of the family that had taken Michael in when he was a boy. Even as warmth had stolen through her, she had realized that she was heading down a very dangerous road. Being accepted by the obviously warmhearted Mrs. Havilcek was a far cry from having Michael indicate that he wanted her in his life in any meaningful way.

She had tried to remain on the fringes of the family's reunion, staying silent and unobtrusive so that no one else would get the idea that she and Michael were a couple. Clearly his foster mother had jumped to that conclusion, and that was likely to be awkward enough.

Kelly had spent the rest of the weekend trying to think of some way to extricate herself from the visit to Ryan's Place, but nothing came to mind—probably because the truth was that she wanted to be there to see how the Havilceks and Devaneys blended together, and whether Michael was at ease among them.

Even so, on Tuesday she attempted to make an excuse as she and Michael were finishing his therapy session. The two hours hadn't gone especially well, and he was in a particularly foul temper because of it. She probably should have waited to broach the subject of Friday night until his mood improved, but she wanted to get it over with.

"One more thing," she said as she gathered up her equipment. "I've been thinking about Friday, and I don't think that's going to work for me."

Michael's gaze shot up, a surprising display of alarm in his eyes. "Why not?"

"It's just not. I..." The lie faltered on her lips, but she sucked in a breath and managed to get it out. "I have a date."

He regarded her curiously. Suddenly his anger seemed to fade. "Is that so?" he said mildly. "Can't be much of a date, if you didn't even remember it when the subject of Friday night came up on Saturday." His gaze narrowed. "Or did you make it after that?"

Kelly hated the faint hint of contempt in his eyes at the possibility that she was breaking her plans with him to go out with someone who'd issued a later invitation. "No, of course not," she insisted, unwilling to carry the lie to that extreme. She didn't want him to dislike her. Nor did she want to destroy the fragile trust they were building. She merely wanted to protect her heart. "It was on my calendar. I'd just forgotten about it."

"Is this date with a man?" he asked.

Kelly studied him curiously. He'd almost sounded jealous, but that couldn't possibly be. Or could it? She decided to play out the charade a little longer to try to gauge his reaction. "Don't women usually go out with men?" she asked. "Besides, my private life is none of your concern. We set up the ground rules weeks ago."

He sighed at that. "Technically, no," he agreed. "But this family thing is important to me. I thought you understood that I want you to be there."

"Of course I understand that it's important, but you don't need me there," she said, instantly feeling guilty for trying to wriggle off the hook. "Look at this another way. If I stay away, we'll avoid all sorts of potentially embarrassing questions."

"Such as?"

"What I'm doing at what should be a very private meeting between the Havilceks and the Devaneys," she explained. "That's likely to stir up all sorts of speculation."

Michael suddenly grinned. "So that's it," he said as if he'd just discovered some huge secret. "You're scared my mother's about to start making wedding plans. You should have thought of that before you started asking her for the recipe for all my favorite dishes."

She frowned at his obvious amusement. Maybe it was a big joke to him, but it wasn't to her. "Aren't you worried about that?"

"Not particularly."

"Why?" she asked, bewildered by the fact that he wasn't the least bit concerned.

"Because my mother is basically harmless. And if she does start getting any crazy ideas, I'll set her straight. It's not a big deal, Kelly. I can handle my mother."

"Yeah, I could see that on Saturday," she said dryly.

He laughed. "Okay, I can *usually* handle my mother." His expression sobered. "Come on, Kelly, tell the truth. You don't really have a date, do you?"

Continuing to lie was obviously pointless. Apparently she wasn't all that good at it. "No," she finally admitted with a sigh.

"Then come."

"Why is my being there so important to you?"

Now it was his turn to look vaguely bewildered. "It just is," he said finally. "I feel more..." He paused, searching for a word. "I feel more normal when you're around."

The explanation left her more confused than ever. "Normal how?"

He looked away as if he were almost embarrassed to make the admission. "You don't get that expression in your eyes when you look at me that everyone else gets," he said.

Kelly was beginning to get the picture. "No pity?"

"Exactly. And you don't let me off the hook when I'm behaving badly. Everyone else does, as if I deserve a pass because I'm in this damned chair. That's the last thing I need. I need to be held accountable for my actions. I need *you* right now."

Kelly swallowed hard against the tide of emotion rising in her throat. Michael's admission that he needed her—that he needed anyone—took her breath away. It was a huge breakthrough for a man who'd probably gone through his whole life trying to convince himself that he didn't need anyone. How could she possibly turn him down after that?

"What time?" she asked, resigned.

As he realized what she was saying, a smile spread slowly across his face. "Pick me up at seven?"

Kelly almost agreed, then recalled that he'd told his family to meet at the pub at six-thirty. "Isn't that a little late?"

He gave her a rueful look at having been caught. "I was hoping they'd get all the introductions out of the way before I got there."

She shook her head. "I don't think so. I'll pick you up at six-fifteen, and no dillydallying. Be outside and ready to go. I'll remind you of that when I'm here on Thursday."

Michael laughed, clearly in a much better frame of mind now that she'd caved in to his request. "Yes, ma'am."

Impulsively she went back and touched his cheek. The faint stubble was rough against her palm. His heat and masculinity drew her as no other man's ever had. It was getting harder and harder to go on with the charade that she was immune to him. "It's going to be okay, you know."

He placed his hand over hers and held it in place. "With you there, something tells me it will be."

Michael still wasn't used to Kelly having her hands all over him. It didn't seem to faze her, so he knew he shouldn't let it bother him, but it did. In fact, it was driving him crazy. As if worrying about Friday night weren't bad enough, today he couldn't seem to keep his thoughts from straying to what it would be like if Kelly's touches were a little—okay, *a lot*—less impersonal.

"How do you do it?" he asked finally when it felt as if he might explode if she stroked her hands over his thigh one more time. He'd spent the past few weeks trying to hide the fact that he was in a perpetual state of arousal when she was around and it was beginning to get to him.

"Do what?" she asked, sounding oddly distant.

"The massage thing."

"I took classes."

He glanced back over his shoulder and frowned. "Not what I meant, and you know it."

She met his gaze, then looked hastily away, her cheeks suddenly rosy.

"Doesn't it bother you?" he persisted.

"It's my job," she said, her tone as prim as someone's elderly maiden aunt. "You're a client."

"I'm also a man," he reminded her. Some wicked instinct had him rolling over to prove the point. He was thoroughly aroused…and that was despite a concerted attempt to remain completely disconnected from the massage.

Kelly's attention was immediately drawn to the evidence. She swallowed hard, then deliberately looked away. Michael tried to gauge her reaction. It had almost seemed as if she was more fascinated—maybe even secretly pleased—than embarrassed. Maybe she wasn't as immune as he'd thought.

"Look, I…" Her words dwindled off.

He reached out and clasped her hand in his. "I don't mean to make you uncomfortable. I really don't.

Actually, I was curious about how you remain detached from what you're doing.''

She met his gaze. ''The truth?''

''Of course.''

''The issue has never really come up before.''

''Before?'' he repeated, a certain measure of gloating creeping into his voice. ''Meaning it has with me? You aren't unaffected by touching me?''

She pulled away. ''Don't sound so blasted pleased with yourself. We really shouldn't be having this conversation. It s inappropriate and totally unprofessional on my part. Besides, we had an agreement.''

She was so clearly dismayed that he instantly backed off. Besides, he had the answer he wanted. The attraction wasn't as one-sided as he'd imagined. Satisfied with that knowledge, he rolled back on his stomach and rested his head on his arms. ''I'll drop it, then,'' he murmured.

''Thank you.''

''But don't be surprised if it comes up again tomorrow night when you're not on the clock.''

Her hands on his leg stilled. ''Michael!'' she protested weakly.

''Kelly!'' he responded, teasing.

She sighed heavily. ''What am I going to do about you?''

''An intriguing question,'' he told her. ''Let's put that on the agenda for tomorrow night, too.''

''You realize if these topics come up tomorrow night, we might never actually make it to the pub?''

He hid his grin. ''Definitely an added bonus,'' he conceded.

She smacked his uninjured leg. ''Forget it, Deva-

ney. I'm not providing you with an excuse to get out
of introducing your families to each other.''

''Oh, well, it was worth a try,'' he said with an air
of resignation.

And getting Kelly to admit that she was not oblivious to the effects of these massages had definitely
been a side benefit. Of course, it was also likely to
fuel his own fantasies so that he wouldn't get a minute's rest between tonight and tomorrow. He figured
the sacrifice of a little sleep was worth it.

Kelly was a nervous wreck on Friday night. She
told herself she was worried for Michael's sake, that
she merely wanted everything to go well, but it was
more than that. The entire conversation they'd had
about the impact of her massages on him had been
disconcerting at best. His assurance that he intended
to get into the subject again tonight the instant they
were alone had her feeling edgy with anticipation of
an entirely different sort.

She had been stunned when he'd revealed that he
was thoroughly aroused. Stunned and, she was willing
to admit, thrilled that she could have that kind of impact on a man she'd been convinced didn't think of
her as a woman at all. There was little question now
that Michael saw her as a desirable grown-up, not a
kid. But what would he do about it? Would he do the
noble thing and ignore it because of his friendship
with her brother and her role as his therapist? She
hoped not. She'd been waiting far too long for him to
notice her.

Of course, that wistful thought lasted only the
length of time it took to say ''lost license.'' She could
just imagine what Moira would have to say if Kelly

revealed that there was anything the least bit provocative about her contact with a client.

She should get a grip, she told herself sternly, and tell Michael he had to do the same. Or she should quit. One or the other. She certainly couldn't let things continue as they had been, not if she valued her professional reputation.

But the prospect of not seeing Michael on a regular basis was inconceivable. He'd come to mean too much to her. Her childish infatuation was developing into something far more important. Something she had to ignore, though, if she wanted to see him through his rehabilitation. And she did want that. She wanted to be there when his leg was strong and he was finally able to walk again. Which meant she was going to have to push her personal feelings for him aside and pretend they didn't exist, no matter how badly he tormented her.

When she arrived Friday night to pick him up, he was dutifully waiting for her outside, despite the fact that the temperature had dropped and there was a threat of snow in the damp air.

"Are you crazy?" she demanded as she got out to open the door and help him into the car. "Why didn't you wait inside?"

"You told me six-fifteen and that I wasn't to dilly-dally," he reminded her.

"And you always do what I say?"

He gave her his most winning smile, the one that made her heart flip over. "I try."

Kelly noticed that he was able to transfer himself to the car a bit more easily than he could the previous weekend. He was actually able to put a little weight on his bad leg. When he was settled, she put the wheelchair in the back, then got back behind the wheel and glanced over at him.

"You ready?"

"No."

She grinned at his sour expression. "Too bad."

"We could run away to the Caribbean. Spend a month or two in the sun getting a tan," he suggested, regarding her seriously. "My treat."

"As much as the possibility of spending a few days on a beach where the temperature is at least fifty degrees warmer than it is here appeals to me, I'm afraid I'll have to say no to that, too."

"You're no fun," he accused.

His words, clearly spoken in jest, hit a raw nerve. "So I've been told," she said, unable to keep the old hurt out of her voice.

Her response clearly startled him. His gaze narrowed. "What idiot said a thing like that?"

"The last man I dated."

Something in his expression turned dark and dangerous. "He hurt you, didn't he?"

"Well, it's never pleasant being told that one is a bore," she said, trying to make light of it.

It wasn't that Phil Cavanaugh had devastated her. She hadn't cared enough about him for his opinion to matter that much, but she had been shaken. It had made her question if that was why no relationship she'd been in had lasted more than a few months. Had Phil been speaking the truth? Was that the conclusion her other dates had eventually reached?

"Why would he say such a thing?" Michael prodded.

"Look, just forget about it," she said. "It's not important. I shouldn't have mentioned it."

"You mentioned it because even though I was joking, I apparently struck a nerve. Now, tell me," he ordered, "what gave this jerk the idea that you weren't much fun? Was there some specific incident, or was he just insulting you on general principle?"

Kelly had never examined that awful exchange from that exact perspective before. She considered Michael's question thoughtfully. It hadn't been an out-of-the-blue comment on her personality at all. Phil had made the accusation when she'd refused to join him at a nightclub for swinging singles, who enjoyed sharing their partners. She'd been stunned that he'd asked in the first place. He'd professed to be shocked by her refusal. Obviously they hadn't known each other at all. For months afterward she'd struggled to figure out why he'd ever thought she would go along with such an idea. She'd refused every invitation, terrified that the man who asked had the same low impression of her morals that Phil had had.

Suddenly she felt Michael's hand cover hers.

"Kelly, what happened?" he asked, regarding her with concern. "I really want to know."

And oddly enough, she found that she wanted to tell him, but how to explain it so that she didn't feel even dirtier than she had that night? "He made a rather insulting suggestion about how we could spend an evening and I turned him down," she said finally, skirting the specifics.

"Some men don't take rejection well," he noted.

Her lips twitched slightly. If only it were that simple. "As I recall, not five minutes ago you made the same comment when I turned your invitation down."

"Yes, but I was joking and you knew it." He studied her intently. "You did know it, didn't you?"

"Honestly, yes, but that didn't stop me from having an instant of déjà vu."

"I'm sorry. Not that I don't think running away to the Caribbean with you to be an excellent idea, but I was only trying to buy myself some time." He lifted his wrist, looked at his watch, and a triumphant grin spread across his face. "Which I have successfully done."

Kelly glanced at the clock on the dashboard and realized it was indeed after six-thirty. All thoughts of the slimy Phil Cavanaugh fled. She scowled at Michael. "You rat!"

"At least acknowledge that I'm a clever rat," he teased.

"Not a chance. I intend to tell everyone who'll listen that we're late because you're not only sneaky, but you're also a total chicken."

He regarded her with mock ferocity. "You wouldn't dare," he said direly.

"Watch me."

He didn't say another word as she started the car and drove the short distance to Ryan's Place, but as soon as she'd parked and come around the car to help him into his wheelchair, he snagged her hand and pulled her closer.

"I know one way to stop you," he said, amusement threading through his voice.

"Oh? How?"

"Like this." He gave a firm tug that had her tumbling into his lap. His mouth covered hers in a kiss that robbed her of breath and definitely cut off both thoughts and speech. Her pulse was scrambling by the time he released her.

She stood up shakily, cleared her throat and regarded him through dazed eyes. "You won't do that, though," she said, her voice unsteady.

"I won't?"

"No," she said with confidence. "It would stir up too many questions."

He laughed. "Do you honestly think I'm afraid of a few questions? Especially when the trade-off is a chance to kiss you thoroughly? Sweetheart, remember that I've been trained to withstand the worst kind of torture without breaking."

Kelly didn't like the gleam in his eye. She realized suddenly that he meant exactly what he was saying. He would kiss her into silence and enjoy every outrageous minute of it.

So would she, but that was another issue entirely, and she was not about to share that little tidbit of information with him.

For once, kissing Kelly had served a purpose other than completely and fruitlessly turning him on. He was feeling downright cheerful and relaxed when they finally went into his brother's pub. Unfortunately, his sister-in-law was the first to spot them. Maggie was on the two of them like a hummingbird after nectar.

"My, my, my," she said, subjecting both of them to a thorough survey. "Rosy cheeks, avoiding looking at each other. Hmm, what could it mean?"

"Nothing," Kelly insisted, her cheeks burning an even deeper shade of pink.

Maggie's gaze settled on Michael. "You going to lie to me, too?"

He grinned. "Not a chance. I know better."

Maggie patted his back. "Good man," she said approvingly. She winked at Kelly. "Fibbing is a waste of time, anyway. I saw you two through the front window. It was quite a show, at least until that kiss pretty much fogged up the window. Then I had to rely on my imagination to guess what was going on.''

"Oh, God," Kelly whispered, obviously embarrassed. "Did everyone see?"

Maggie wrapped a consoling arm around her shoulders. "Only me and Ryan," she said, then added, "and the people at the table by the door."

Kelly whirled in that direction, then groaned when she saw it was Michael's folks. His mother seemed especially pleased by what she'd observed. His father was merely studying the two of them with a speculative look.

Maggie laughed. "Definitely a fascinated audience, am I right?"

Michael shook his head at Maggie's obvious pleasure in their discomfort. Ryan definitely had his hands full with her. Michael couldn't decide if he pitied him or envied him. Add in Caitlyn, and the balance definitely tilted toward envy.

"I gather you've met the Havilceks," he said to Maggie.

"Yes," she responded cheerfully. "Why don't you two go on and join them? Ryan's going to move some more tables together in a minute. Sean and Deanna will be here soon."

"And your folks?" Michael asked.

"They decided to wait until another time. They didn't want to intrude."

"Which I shouldn't be doing, either," Kelly said, suddenly backing away as if she were about to make a break for the door. "Michael, I'm sure someone here will give you a lift home. I'll see you tomorrow for your therapy session.''

She moved quickly, but even confined to his damnable chair, Michael was faster. He blocked her way and waited until her nervous gaze finally met his.

"I thought we'd settled this earlier in the week," he chided. "I want you here."

"But what must they think of me?" she whispered. "Kissing you right out there in public. What was I thinking?"

"Frankly, I don't think either one of us were doing much thinking," he retorted. "And for the record, this time I kissed you, not the other way around."

"In the grand scheme of things, I think that qualifies as a pretty puny technicality," she retorted.

Suddenly his mother's voice cut through their debate. "When are you two going to stop bickering and get over here?" she asked.

"My master calls," Michael said. "Are you going to dare to defy her?"

For an instant, he thought Kelly might do just that, but then she sighed and visibly squared her shoulders. "Let's go," she said. "But just so you know, you are going to pay for this. I have an exercise that will bring you to your knees."

Michael grinned at her. "An intriguing concept. I can hardly wait," he said, his tone deliberately wicked.

He noticed Kelly was still sputtering in indignation as she swept past him and went to join his parents. All things considered, the evening was off to a much better start than he'd anticipated.

Chapter Eight

It took less than an hour for Kelly to forget about how thoroughly flustered she'd been by Michael's kiss and Maggie's teasing. The heat she'd expected to keep her cheeks a permanent shade of embarrassed pink finally cooled, and she began to relax. After all, this evening wasn't really about her at all. It was about the Havilceks and the Devaneys getting to know each other.

Although Michael had clearly dreaded the entire occasion and she'd been expecting it to be awkward, they'd both evidently forgotten about the warmth exuded by his foster mother and his sister-in-law. Doris Havilcek and Maggie Devaney were like a couple of cruise ship social directors determined to see that everyone had a good time. Introductions were accompanied by anecdotes designed to provide insight and provoke good-natured laughter. Kelly was in awe of them, and more than a little envious.

So, apparently, was Michael. She turned to find him watching his foster mother with a dazed expression. Leaning close, she noted, "She's an amazing woman, isn't she?"

"Even more so than I realized," he admitted. "I thought she'd feel threatened by having my brothers suddenly thrust into the middle of our lives, but she's not. She's simply opening that generous heart of hers and adding them to her family as if they'd just been rediscovered after a long absence. And my dad and sisters are following her lead."

"I'm glad for you," Kelly told him sincerely. "It would have been hard if they hadn't gotten along. I'm sure you would have felt torn."

Before Michael could respond, Sean moved into the vacant seat on his other side. "You really lucked out in the foster family department," Sean told him. "The Havilceks are terrific people."

Michael nodded. "No question about it."

"I've tried to get my last foster family in here to spend some time with Ryan and Maggie, but they're not much interested. Deanna and I go by to see them once in a while, but I always have the feeling if we stopped going they'd hardly notice. They're good people, but they've moved on. I always had the feeling that they knew there would always be another foster kid waiting just around the corner, so they tried not to get too attached to any of us."

Sean shrugged as if it didn't matter to him, but Kelly could see that it did. And it must be even harder on Ryan, who'd never stayed with the same foster family for more than a few months at a time. There was no one from his past to whom he felt the slightest sentimental attachment.

"Well, it looks to me as if you can all count on being part of the Havilcek clan from now on," Kelly told Sean. "Mrs. Havilcek will see to that."

Sean grinned. "Fine by me. I've heard about her apple pie."

Ryan joined them. "Did I hear somebody mention apple pie? Who's baking?"

Michael shook his head and regarded his big brother with amusement. "You'd think that a man who owns his own pub wouldn't have any trouble getting all the food he wants."

"Rory is a genius when it comes to cooking up an Irish stew or anything else he learned in Dublin, but he's yet to master an American apple pie," Ryan said with apparent regret. "Maggie's offered to teach him, but he's vowed to leave the day she starts trying to take over his kitchen the way she's taken over the rest of this place. Now, when my Caitlyn gets a little older, it'll be another story. That daughter of mine has our Rory wound around her little finger. She could sit in the kitchen all day long, banging on his favorite pots and pans with a spoon, and he'd never complain about the noise or the scratches."

"Speaking of Caitlyn, where is my niece tonight?" Michael asked.

"Upstairs with the baby-sitter and, with any luck, sound asleep," Ryan said.

"As is my son," Sean said. "Though I imagine he's playing video games rather than sleeping. He told us he wasn't a baby like Caitlyn, so Deanna bribed him to stay out of our hair for a few hours. I think Kevin's destined for a top-level management career in business. He's already a tough negotiator. Deanna and I come out on the losing end more than I'd like to admit.''

Kelly listened with fascination as the talk centering on the kids went on for several minutes. Apparently both Ryan and Sean had been able to put their own bad experiences with abandonment behind them and had taken to parenting like the proverbial ducks to water. She wondered if Michael would eventually do the same. Because he'd been younger and because he'd landed with the Havilceks right at the beginning, he seemed to have fewer issues than his older brothers had had growing up.

And yet, she sensed that Michael still had moments when he felt like an outsider. His failure to call the Havilceks the minute he returned to Boston was evidence of it. Though he'd made perfectly rational excuses for that, Kelly wondered if he hadn't been just a little bit afraid of how they would perceive him now that he was no longer going to be a strong, able-bodied hero. He should have known better, but there had to be lingering insecurities from being abandoned by his own parents. How could there not be?

She snapped back to the present when she heard Ryan mention the search for the rest of the Devaneys.

''The investigator says he has a lead. It's not a sure thing, but he's found a Patrick Devaney up in Maine,'' Ryan told them. ''He thinks it could be one of the twins. The age is about right. They'd be nearly twenty-six by now.''

Sean's expression darkened. ''Is he going up there to check it out?''

''Actually, I thought maybe we should be the ones to go,'' Ryan said slowly.

"Forget it!" Sean said with surprising heat. "Finding the two of you has been great, but I've been giving it a lot of thought. I think that's going to be it for me."

Ryan turned to Michael, who looked as if he might object, as well. "Do you feel the same way?" Ryan asked him.

Kelly wasn't sure what she expected Michael to say or even what was right. This was an incredibly delicate situation, and clearly each of the brothers was coming at it from an entirely different perspective. And the twins might very well bring about a reunion between the three brothers and their biological parents.

"I need to think about it," Michael said, his earlier good mood suddenly vanishing. He glanced worriedly toward the Havilceks, as if he feared they might overhear the conversation. When he turned back to Ryan, he said, "This is a big step. We're getting closer to our parents. This guy's not going anywhere, right?"

"It doesn't sound like it," Ryan said.

"Then let me and Sean give it some more thought and we'll talk later, okay?"

"Sure. No problem," Ryan said. "Trust me, I've got mixed feelings about this myself. Not so much about finding Patrick and Daniel. I think that would be great. But like you said, if they're going to lead us to our folks, I'm not sure how I feel about that."

"I know exactly how I feel," Sean said bitterly. "If they haven't bothered to look for us in all these years, it's their loss."

"We don't know they haven't looked," Michael suggested quietly.

Sean scowled at him. "Of course we do. If they

had, they would have found us. It didn't take Ryan all that long to track me down, and the two of us were able to find you. It's not as if any of us had changed our names and moved to the far ends of the earth.''

"Sean, believe me, you're not saying anything I haven't thought myself,'' Ryan responded. "But maybe none of us will really be at peace with the past until we know the truth about what happened. Maggie's forced me to see that.'' He patted Sean on the back. "But it's up to you. You two get back to me once you've thought it over. I'd better get back to the bar for a bit.''

Ryan started away, then turned back to Michael. "By the way,'' he began casually, "there's a guy who comes in here once in a while who runs a fleet of charter boats. I'd like you to meet him sometime.''

Kelly watched Michael's already stormy expression turn even darker.

"Oh? What does that have to do with me?'' Michael asked.

"A guy with your background has to have an interest in boats, right? You must have been trained on every kind imaginable,'' Ryan responded. "I just thought you'd have a lot in common. And he's told me he has a hard time finding captains who know the equipment.''

"The day won't come when I'll steer a bunch of damned tourists around Boston Harbor,'' Michael said heatedly.

Ryan shrugged as if his response were of no consequence. "It was just an idea. What would it hurt to talk to him? Add that to your list of things to think about, okay?''

He walked away without waiting for Michael's response.

Sean gave Michael a searching look, then sighed. "I think I'll go upstairs and check on the kids," he said.

After his brothers had gone, Michael faced Kelly with a troubled expression. "So, what do you think about this search of Ryan's?"

She noticed he didn't mention the job prospect Ryan had dangled in front of him. Apparently he really had dismissed it out of hand.

"It's really none of my business," she said finally.

"And that's stopped you from forming an opinion?" Michael asked skeptically.

"Hardly," she admitted with a rueful grin.

"Tell me."

"I understand why all of you would hesitate, but I think Maggie's right. I'm sure every one of you has wondered all these years why your parents disappeared and left you behind. I can't even begin to imagine what kind of impact that's had on your lives." She searched his face, trying to gauge how he was responding, but his expression was neutral. "Come on, Michael, isn't it better to find out the truth and put it behind you, once and for all?"

"Then the answer's pretty much black-and-white to you," he concluded. "You think we should go and see if this Patrick is one of the twins?"

"Yes, I do."

Michael's expression turned thoughtful. "Think about this, though. He was barely two when everything happened. He might not even remember that he had brothers. He and Daniel and our parents might have had this tight-knit, perfectly happy family all these years. How's he going to feel if three of us show up out of the blue and announce it was all a fraud?''

"It wasn't a fraud," Kelly replied. "It was simply *his* experience as a Devaney versus the ones each of you had."

"But it could forever alter his trust in our parents. Do we have the right to do that?" He seemed genuinely tormented by the question.

"You know what I think? I think it's amazing that you're thinking of his feelings at all. That's something a big brother would do. How can he not want to know that he has three older brothers who care deeply about him despite years and years of separation?"

Michael shook his head. "I think you're being overly optimistic. I think he's going to resent the hell out of us for coming in and destroying his world."

"Then you'll apologize and let him go on just as he has been."

"You're being naive, Kelly," Michael accused her. "It doesn't work that way. The damage will have been done."

Kelly could see his point, but that was only one scenario. She pointed out another. "What if all these years, he has remembered having older brothers?" she asked. "What if he's always felt as if a part of his life was missing? Are you ready to deny him the answers he needs to feel complete?"

Michael frowned at her questions. "If only we could predict which way it was going to go," he said plaintively.

She put her hand over his and squeezed. "We can't. We can only calculate the risks and make the best choice possible. No one should understand that better

than you do. You've made a career out of taking cal-
culated risks.''

"Yeah, but those are the kind of risks I understand,'' he said.

"They're life-and-death risks,'' she countered.

"And this isn't?'' he asked wryly.

"Certainly not in the same way,'' she insisted.

"Remind me to have this conversation with you
again when your entire world's been turned upside
down,'' he said.

Little did he know that it already had been…on the
day he'd come back into her life.

Despite Kelly's opinion that things would turn out
all right, Michael was still feeling uneasy about this
search for the rest of his biological family. On the one
hand, it had turned out okay when Ryan and Sean had
found him, but on the other, he sensed it was going
to be very different with the twins.

As for finding his parents, he wasn't even ready to
go there yet. He was not as bitter toward them as Ryan
and Sean obviously were. He simply didn't care much
one way or the other. That was a hornet's nest he
didn't particularly want to disturb, but more and more
it was growing inevitable that he would have to unless
they called a halt to the search now. Whatever they
did, they needed to be united, because all their lives
were going to be affected. He honestly didn't know
which decision was the right one.

There was one person, though, whose opinion he
trusted more than anyone else's when it came to matters of family—his foster mother. Impulsively, the
minute his therapy session ended and Kelly had gone,
he called a cab and went over to the Havilceks. The

fact that his mother would be in the midst of her Saturday baking wasn't entirely coincidental.

It grated on him that he had to ask the cab driver to go up to the house and let his mother know to let him in through the garage, but the beaming smile on her face negated that momentary humiliation. She shivered as she waited for him just inside the garage.

"Come on in here, Michael," she said briskly. "It's freezing out there this morning. What brings you by? It's too early for the pies to be out of the oven, you know."

He regarded her slyly. "But not the cinnamon rolls, I'll bet."

She grinned. "With milk or coffee?"

"Milk, of course."

She waited until he was settled at the kitchen table before sitting opposite him, her expression suddenly serious. "What's on your mind, Michael? Did you and Kelly have a fight last night?"

Startled by the question, Michael paused with a forkful of gooey cinnamon roll halfway to his mouth. "No. Why would you think that?"

"Something changed during the evening. You were so clearly happy when you came in, but when you left, you both looked…" She hesitated, then said, "Serious, I guess. I thought something might have happened."

He let the cinnamon roll practically dissolve on his tongue as he studied his mother. "You like her, don't you? It would really bother you if we'd fought."

"Well, of course I like her. The two of you seem good together, but it's your feelings that count."

He ought to be pleased by the assessment, but instead it made him uneasy. "We're not dating, you know. She's my therapist."

His mother grinned. "If you say so, dear."

Michael frowned. "I do."

"Then you might consider not kissing her quite so enthusiastically," she teased. "It could give people, including Kelly, the wrong impression."

"I'll try to keep that in mind," he said wryly.

His mother studied him intently. "Okay, then, if you didn't come to talk about Kelly, why are you here?"

"You and the cinnamon rolls aren't excuse enough?"

"We certainly could be, and I'd be flattered if we were, but I have my doubts."

"Do you realize how disconcerting it is to have a mother who can virtually read your mind?"

"I can be vague if you'd prefer it," she offered.

"Hardly. Okay, here it is. Ryan thinks he may have found one of our younger brothers in Maine. He wants all of us to go up and check it out."

She nodded slowly. "I see. And you don't want to go?"

"It's not that. I just keep trying to put myself in Patrick's place. He was little more than a baby when the family split up. For all we know, he's lived happily ever after, and now here we come barging in to tell him that his idyllic situation cost the rest of us a family."

She regarded him knowingly. "Are you so sure it's Patrick you're worried about?"

"Of course."

"Michael," she chided in the tone she used when

GET FREE BOOKS and a FREE GIFT WHEN YOU PLAY THE...

Just scratch off the silver box with a coin. Then check below to see the gifts you get!

SLOT MACHINE GAME!

YES! I have scratched off the silver box. Please send me the 2 free Silhouette Special Edition® books and gift for which I qualify. I understand I am under no obligation to purchase any books, as explained on the back of this card.

235 SDL DRRW
(S-SE-01/03)

335 SDL DRRG

FIRST NAME

LAST NAME

ADDRESS

APT.#

CITY

STATE/PROV.

ZIP/POSTAL CODE

7	7	7	**Worth TWO FREE BOOKS plus a BONUS Mystery Gift!**
🍒	🍒	🍒	**Worth TWO FREE BOOKS!**
♣	♣	♣	**Worth ONE FREE BOOK!**
🔔	🔔	🍒	**TRY AGAIN!**

Visit us online at www.eHarlequin.com

DETACH AND MAIL CARD TODAY!

she thought one of her children wasn't being entirely forthright.

He frowned at the unspoken accusation. "Okay, maybe I'm the one with the problem. I lucked out. I wound up with the best family a boy could ask for, but a tiny part of me resents the fact that the twins got to keep our biological parents and the rest of us were sent away. I don't think I even realized how much I resented it until last night when Ryan said his investigator had a lead on Patrick."

"You know that none of this was Patrick's fault," his mother said. "Any more than it was yours or Ryan's or Sean's."

"Yes, but…" He sighed. "You know what I really don't get is why Ryan's suddenly so anxious to find the twins and our parents. He should be the angriest of all, and, deep down, I think he is. It's Maggie who's convinced him to do this."

"Maybe he's simply wise enough to realize he'll never let go of that anger until he has the whole story."

"Then you think we should go," he concluded, knowing that was exactly what he'd expected her to say when he'd come here. Maybe he'd wanted her blessing even more than he'd wanted her advice.

She rested her hand against his cheek. "Michael, I love you as much as if you were one of my own," she said quietly. "But this is not my decision. You need to listen to your heart."

That was going to be hard to do for a man who'd grown used to ignoring anything his heart had to say, especially if it happened to be the least bit inconvenient. He'd always thought of himself as a man of cool actions, not emotion.

"And while you're at it," she added slyly, "you might see what your heart has to say about Kelly. You could be surprised."

"Careful," he teased. "Some men might find your meddling annoying."

"Not the smart ones," she retorted. "Now, shall I turn off the oven and give you a lift home? Or can you stay for dinner?"

"Not tonight. I have some thinking to do. And don't worry about the lift. I'll call a cab."

"Let me do it," she said, already moving toward the phone.

Michael shrugged into his jacket and jockeyed the wheelchair into the garage.

"I'm not opening that door yet," his mother warned. "The cab company said it would be at least ten minutes. I wish you'd just let me take you."

"This is fine, Mom."

"One of these days you'll be driving yourself places again," she said with confidence. It was the first time she'd ventured any sort of comment about his future.

"I hope so."

"I know so," she said emphatically. "Now give me a kiss." She bent down and accepted his kiss. "I love you."

"I love you, too."

She regarded him intently. "Finding your biological parents won't diminish that."

He smiled. "I know that."

"Just thought I'd mention it, in case it was on your mind."

"Have I told you lately how incredible you are and how lucky I am to have you in my life?"

"You never had to say it," she said, though there were tears in her eyes. "Mothers can usually see straight into their children's hearts."

"You can," he told her. "I'm not so sure Kathleen Devaney could."

"You won't know that until you see her again."

Michael sighed. "Will you be disappointed in me if I decide against it?"

"I could never be disappointed in you as long as you make your choice for the right reasons," she said with conviction.

The arrival of the taxi saved him from having to think about what his mother would consider valid reasons for leaving things just as they were.

But finding Kelly waiting on his doorstep pretty much guaranteed that he wasn't off the hook for the day, after all.

Michael didn't look especially overjoyed to see her, Kelly concluded as he exited a taxi and made his way up the walk to where she waited. She wasn't sure what had drawn her back to his place after she'd finished with her last client. Maybe it had been his distraction during their morning session. More likely, it was the uneasy conversation they'd had the night before. She'd avoided asking about the search that morning, but it had clearly been on his mind. He'd hardly said two words to her during the entire session.

"What brings you back?" he asked as he maneuvered the wheelchair past her and into the foyer. "Did you forget something?"

"No." She'd been waiting for a half hour and in all that time she hadn't managed to come up with a halfway plausible excuse for returning aside from wanting to see him. "If you're busy, I can leave."

"I'm not busy," he said. "Are you hungry? We could order a pizza or something."

She was surprised by the invitation. "Are you sure you don't mind me being here?"

"To be perfectly honest, I'm glad you're here."

His response startled her, but she didn't want to make too much of it. "Oh?"

"I was over at my mom's. She gave me a lot to think about, but to be frank, I'm not looking forward to all the soul-searching required."

"If you're looking for a distraction, maybe I should go rent us a couple of videos, too."

He grinned. "Perfect."

"Action, romance or comedy?"

"What do you think?"

"One action movie for you, one chick flick for me," she concluded. "That's only fair."

He nodded. "What do you want on your pizza? I'll order while you're gone."

"Nothing slimy."

Michael laughed. "Besides anchovies, what exactly does that exclude?"

"Onions and mushrooms."

"Fine by me. I'll get half pepperoni and half sausage."

"You have beers or sodas?"

"Plenty of both," he confirmed.

"Then I'll be right back." She started down the walk, then turned back. "When was the last time you went to the movies, just so I don't get something you've already seen."

"The last movie I saw was *Lethal Weapon*."

"Which one?"

He stared at her blankly. "There was more than one? Movies weren't something I paid any attention to once I hit my teens. I was too wrapped up in sports."

Kelly laughed. "I can see you have a lot of catching up to do."

It took her less than twenty minutes to pick up *Lethal Weapon II*, along with *Die Hard* and *Pearl Harbor*, and for her, the romantic comedy *Return to Me*, which she'd already seen twice before. She grabbed a package of microwave popcorn at the checkout counter while she was at it.

Back at Michael's, she arrived at the same time as the pizza. She paid the delivery man, then juggled everything and almost dumped it on the floor twice before finally getting the door open.

She noted that Michael had already poured a beer for himself and a soft drink for her and was seated on the sofa with a basketball game on TV. He instinctively started to get up, then fell back with a muttered oath.

"Sorry," he mumbled.

Kelly merely nodded, took the pizza over to the coffee table, then held up the movie selections. "You pick first."

He pointed to the Bruce Willis film. "Somehow testosterone goes better with pizza and beer."

"A matter of opinion," she noted, but she slipped it into the tape player and sat down beside him.

As requested, the movie was noisy and filled with action, so no conversation was required, but Kelly still felt as if Michael was holding something back. As soon as it was over, rather than slipping a second tape into the machine, she turned to him.

"Are you sure you don't want to talk about whatever's on your mind?"

He leveled a look at her and slowly shook his head. "I'd rather do this," he said, reaching for her.

Kelly sighed and murmured, "Me, too," just as his mouth covered hers.

Chapter Nine

The kiss did what nothing else had been able to do. It drove all thoughts of the search for the rest of the Devaneys from Michael's head. All that mattered was the silky brush of Kelly's lips across his, the intoxicating heat that curled through him like a slug of fine Scotch, and the thundering of his heart. For a few minutes, he forgot that he couldn't walk, forgot that his future was filled with uncertainty. All that mattered was here, now and the woman in his arms.

Then, somewhere in the back of his head where his values and conscience resided, he heard the first faint whisper that lust was a poor substitute for deeper feelings. And sex was no way to block out problems that needed to be dealt with.

There was little question that he could spend the next few hours, perhaps even the whole night with Kelly in his bed and his problems on hold. But he'd never used a woman like that before, and he wasn't about to start with one he genuinely liked. He sighed against her delectable lips and slowly released her.

Forehead pressed against hers, he murmured an apology.

"For?" she asked cautiously.

"I keep swearing that I won't do this again."

"Have I complained?"

His lips curved. "No, but you should. There are a million and one reasons why it's a bad idea."

"Name two," she challenged.

"Your professional reputation," he said, tossing her own frequently stated argument back at her. "And the fact that I'm at a crossroads. I have nothing to offer you. Until I figure out who and what I'm going to be now that I'm no longer a SEAL, I have nothing to offer to anyone."

Eyes sparkling with indignation, she frowned at that. "Michael Devaney, if that's not the most ridiculous thing I've ever heard. You don't have to put yourself in harm's way for your country to be a worthwhile human being. The reality is that very few men do what you've been doing the last few years, and most of the rest live perfectly respectable, fulfilling lives with women and children who love them. Are you suggesting that any one of them is less of a man because of what they do or because they don't do what you did?"

"Of course not," he said fiercely. "I would never say anything like that. It's about being able to do what you love, what you're good at. I was good at being a SEAL. I loved it, the same way Ryan loves running his pub or Sean loves being a firefighter. It's about being passionate about something, and then losing it.

We were talking about your professional reputation the other day. That wouldn't matter if your career weren't important to you, right? So, what if you lost it? What if they took your license away? How would you feel?''

Her expression faltered at that. ''I'd hate it,'' she said at once, then added with absolute certainty, ''but I'd get over it and find something else.''

''Just like that?'' Michael asked skeptically. ''You think it's that easy?''

''No, of course it's not easy, and maybe it wouldn't happen overnight, but I wouldn't give up or think my life was over,'' she insisted.

Though he didn't share her belief that she could move on so easily, Michael accepted the fact that she believed it. ''Fair enough,'' he said. ''All I'm saying is that I've only reached the point where I can accept that my life isn't over. That's a long way from knowing what I can do with it.''

''Ryan offered one option the other night,'' she said cautiously. ''You didn't even consider it, did you?''

''No, because it's ridiculous.''

''Why?'' she persisted. ''Because being a charter boat captain is somehow demeaning?''

Michael hesitated. That was part of it, but there was more, something obviously Ryan and Kelly hadn't even considered. ''It's not something I can very well do unless I'm back on my feet.''

''But you will be,'' Kelly said fiercely. ''I believe that with all my heart.''

''I wish I were as confident.''

''Make me a deal, then. *When* you're back on your feet, you'll at least meet your brother's friend.''

As reluctant as he was to do it, he nodded slowly. "Okay, that's fair enough."

"I'll remind you, you know."

He grinned. "I'm sure of it."

She regarded him with a suddenly wistful expression. "Are you saying you can't sleep with me until then, either?"

"I shouldn't," he said emphatically, fighting a whole slew of regrets as he said it. "And I won't."

Kelly tilted her head and gave him a considering look. "Then I hope you won't mind if I bring you a few books on changing careers next time I come by, just in case the charter boat thing doesn't work out."

For the first time in days, Michael laughed. "In other words, you intend to do your best to speed up the process?"

"Yes." She locked gazes with him and ran her thumb across his lower lip. "And be warned, in the meantime, I also intend to make it all but impossible for you to resist me."

Michael's pulse scrambled at the challenge. "Kelly," he protested.

"Save your breath," she said. "That's just the way it's going to be. Until tonight I wasn't absolutely certain you wanted me this way, but now I am."

"And what about all the professional considerations you've mentioned?"

"Easy," she said with a shrug. Her gaze locked with his. "As of tonight, I quit."

He pulled away, shocked by the feeling of desperation that cut through him at her words. "Hey, you can't do that," he protested.

"Sure I can."

"But I need you," he said.

A faint spark of something that might have been satisfaction lit her eyes at his words. "You need a good therapist. It doesn't have to be me. But actually, I have no intention of letting you find one. I'll go on helping you. I just won't let you pay me for it."

"And that makes it okay for you and me to…?" He hesitated over the precise description.

"Have sex," she supplied bluntly, her eyes twinkling at his discomfort.

"Yes, that," he agreed.

She grinned. "It can't hurt. Besides, who's going to turn me in?"

Michael could think of one possibility in particular. Her brother might at least threaten to turn her in to save her from making a huge mistake that would cost her everything. "Bryan," he suggested.

"I'll deal with my brother, not that he's likely to know if you and I are sleeping together."

"Trust me, he'll know," Michael said dryly.

"How?"

"Men always know when their friends are getting lucky."

"Because you all like to brag?"

"No, because we're a whole lot less cranky."

Kelly laughed. "I don't think we need to worry about that in your case. You have lots of excuses to be cranky that have nothing to do with sex. I doubt that will change."

"Thanks," he said, unable to keep a hint of irritation out of his voice.

"Just calling it like I see it."

"I think it's time for you to go," Michael said stiffly.

"It's not that late," she argued.

"Oh, yes, it is."

She regarded him curiously. "Are you afraid you're going to grab me and haul me off to bed right now?"

Michael groaned.

Kelly's expression turned gloating. "That's it, isn't it?"

"A smart woman would stop tempting fate and get out of here before we both regret it."

For what seemed like an eternity, Michael was terrified she was going to refuse. He wasn't sure his willpower was strong enough to withstand even five more minutes of her deliberate teasing.

Finally, her expression thoughtful, she nodded. "You win. For now."

She grabbed her coat and purse, started for the door, then came back and kissed him so thoroughly, he had to wonder if he'd lost his mind when he'd all but kicked her out.

"I'll see you Tuesday bright and early," she called out when she reached the door.

She sounded so blasted cheerful, Michael was tempted to pick up the nearest heavy object and hurl it after her.

But he didn't. He murmured a polite farewell, hit the remote and started another movie. For a long time after she'd gone, he was oblivious to what was playing on the TV screen. Then he noticed that it was a romantic comedy and muttered an oath that could probably be heard down the block.

He shut off the VCR and flipped through the channels until he found a basketball game. Just what he needed, he thought happily, reaching for what was left of his beer. He understood basketball. He understood sweat and competition. He apparently didn't know a thing about women or he would have seen this whole thing with Kelly coming a mile away and he could have gotten out of the damned way.

Kelly sat across the table from her best friend and flinched under Moira's knowing stare. There was no question that this unusual Sunday breakfast was a command performance. The message on her answering machine the night before had made that clear. Now that they were here, she wished Moira would just get it over with. Kelly pushed her eggs around on her plate and waited for the lecture to start. When the minutes dragged on and Moira said nothing, Kelly's nerves finally snapped.

"Just say it," she commanded.

Moira regarded her innocently. "Say what?"

"Whatever you're thinking."

"You don't want to know what I'm thinking."

"Probably not," Kelly murmured morosely, staring at her plate because she couldn't bear to see the censure in the other woman's eyes. "Say it anyway."

"I'm not sure whether to start by asking if you've lost your mind or if you're happy."

"Both," Kelly said.

"Then you are involved with your *client,*" she said, making sure that Kelly understood exactly what was at stake. "I was afraid of that."

"We're not involved," Kelly said. "Not yet, anyway. And I quit last night."

"And that's supposed to make it all right?"

"Look, I know I'm skating on thin ice, professionally speaking, but Michael matters to me. I thought I could keep my personal feelings out of it, but I can't." She shrugged. "So I quit."

"Is he planning to hire another therapist?"

"I don't think so."

"And you intend to go on with his therapy in the meantime?"

Kelly nodded.

Moira met her gaze. "He's that important to you?"

"Yes, he is."

Moira sighed. "How does he feel about you?"

"He wants me," she said. "He doesn't want to, but he does. I figure that's got to be a good start."

"Or a disaster waiting to happen," Moira predicted.

"Come on," Kelly coaxed. "Stop being so gloomy. This could be the best thing that ever happened to me. I've been half in love with Michael Devaney for most of my life. I'm finally getting a chance to see if that's real." She gave Moira a penetrating look. "Are you telling me that if you had the same chance to test things with my brother, you wouldn't grab the opportunity with both hands?"

Moira's pale, lightly freckled complexion flushed a bright red. "Let's leave my feelings for your brother out of this."

It had been an unspoken topic between them for years now. Kelly decided it was past time to put an end to the silence. "Why?" she demanded. "You've been carrying a torch for him forever. Why should both of us continue to deny it?"

"Because it's pointless. Bryan has never given me a second glance. Besides, you're just trying to change the subject to take the heat off of you."

"Yes, I am," Kelly admitted cheerfully. "As for Bryan not giving you a second look, maybe that's because you try to fade into the woodwork whenever he's around. I'll bet he'd take notice if you gave him half a chance. You're a wonderful woman, and you'd be terrific for Bryan. He's a dreamer with his head in the clouds most of the time. You're real. You're grounded. You'd balance each other perfectly.''

"In your opinion," Moira pointed out. "If Bryan thought that, he would have asked me out before now. He's had plenty of opportunities."

"If that isn't the pot calling the kettle black," Kelly chided. "You think it, and you haven't done anything about it. It's pitiful actually. You're shy and he's dense. I could fix that."

Hope stirred in Moira's eyes. "Fix it how?" she asked warily.

Kelly wondered why she hadn't thought to push the two of them together before. Maybe she'd wanted to believe fate would take care of it, but she was discovering lately that fate sometimes needed a helping hand.

"Leave it to me," she told Moira. "What are you doing Friday night? Are you free?"

"I usually do laundry on Friday night."

"Oh, please," Kelly said, dismissing the feeble excuse. "You're free. Meet me at Ryan's Place at seven. It's an Irish pub."

"I know what it is, but why there?"

"Because it's owned by Michael's brother and it's become the Friday night place to be for his family." She gave her friend a wicked grin. "And for my brother."

Moira, who was as confident about most things as any woman Kelly knew, regarded her uncertainly. "I don't know. Won't it be obvious that it's a setup?"

"To my myopic brother?" Kelly scoffed. "Hardly.

Don't even think of arguing with me about this. I'm not taking no for an answer. Seven o'clock, and wear something blue. It's Bryan's favorite color, and you happen to look great in it.''

"Okay, fine. You win," Moira finally agreed. "But I'm only saying yes so I can meet this man who has you taking crazy chances."

"Of course you are," Kelly teased.

"Just because you're trying to fix me up with your brother does not mean you're off the hook," Moira insisted. "I'm still worried about you."

"There's nothing to worry about," Kelly said. "I know exactly what I'm doing where Michael's concerned."

In fact, she was growing more and more certain of it with each passing day.

"So, you'll do it?" Kelly was asking, as she massaged the taut muscles in Michael's calf.

"Do what exactly?" he asked, trying to drag his attention away from the heat that was spreading through him with each strictly professional caress.

"Ask Bryan to join us at the pub Friday night," she explained with obvious impatience. "Weren't you listening to anything I said?"

"Every word," he assured her. Most of them just hadn't registered. It was impossible to concentrate when she was rubbing warm oil into his skin. He'd never thought eucalyptus to be an especially provocative scent, but he was rapidly beginning to change his mind. He forced himself to pay attention to the conversation. "This has something to do with your friend. What was her name again?"

"Moira Brady."

"And Bryan knows her?"

"Yes, but he doesn't pay any attention to her, at least not the way he should."

"So, basically what you're doing is matchmaking, and you want my help?"

"Exactly."

"No way," he said emphatically.

Her hands stilled, and Michael almost regretted being so adamant. Clearly she wasn't pleased with his response.

"Why not?" she asked, her tone suddenly chilly.

"Because men don't meddle in their friends' love lives."

"You don't have to meddle. You just have to ask him to meet us at the pub. It's not as if you've never asked him to join you there before."

"Why can't you ask him? Moira is your friend."

"Because that's too obvious," she said impatiently. "Don't you know anything?"

"Apparently not when it comes to matchmaking, thank God."

This time when her hands stroked his leg, there was something far more sensual than therapeutic about it. Michael responded accordingly. He had to will himself to stop paying attention to those long, lingering strokes and concentrate on counting backward from a thousand. He was getting to be quite good at it.

"Michael, please," she coaxed softly. "It's not such a big deal. There will be a whole crowd of us there, right? It's not as if we're asking him to spend a deadly dull evening all alone with a total toad."

Michael groaned. He was going to say yes eventually and hate himself for it. A few months ago he'd barely remembered Kelly's existence and now he was considering conspiring with her against a man he'd always thought of as his best friend. He suspected traitors could fry in hell for less.

Kelly leaned closer, her breath whispering against his cheek. ''Are you thinking about it?''

''How can I think when you're all over me?'' he muttered irritably.

She laughed. ''I'll take that as a compliment.''

''It wasn't meant that way,'' he groused.

''No, I'm sure it wasn't. But you are going to do this one tiny thing for me, aren't you?''

He rolled over, dragging the sheet with him to cover his unmistakable reaction to her sneaky massage technique. ''I'll do it on one condition.''

''Great!'' she said, obviously pleased.

''Hold on. You haven't heard the condition. I want you to look me in the eye and tell me exactly what put this little scheme into your head. Have you ever fixed your brother up with one of your friends before?''

''No,'' she admitted, looking decidedly uneasy.

''Then why now? Why Moira?''

''I think they'd be perfect for each other,'' she said, sticking to her story.

Michael wasn't buying it, not entirely anyway. ''And you just reached that conclusion this week? Out of the blue? After knowing this Moira for how long?''

''A while,'' she conceded.

''And the inspiration to matchmake never struck you before?''

''Not exactly.''

''Then I have to ask again, why now?''

She frowned at him. ''I sort of owe her.''

''For?''

"Keeping her mouth shut about something," she told him grudgingly.

Suddenly it all became perfectly clear to him. "Moira's the woman who runs the rehab clinic where you work part-time, isn't she? And she found out about the two of us."

He didn't have to see the telltale flush in Kelly's cheeks to know he'd hit the nail on the head. He would have known it by the way she suddenly found a million little things to do to avoid meeting his gaze. When she started lining up her selection of free weights according to size, he shook his head.

"You can't avoid answering me forever," he said.

"Sure I can," she said with obvious bravado.

"So, the price of Moira's silence is a date with your brother," he said, drawing his own conclusions. "And this is a woman you want me to trick him into spending an evening with?"

She scowled at that. "You make it sound so sleazy. It's not that way at all. Moira is a terrific woman. She's just a little shy. She gets all tongue-tied when Bryan is around. And just so we're very clear, this was my idea, not hers."

"But she went along with it," he reminded her.

"Reluctantly. Come on, Michael, what's the harm?"

"There are so many possibilities, I can hardly list them all," he responded.

"Name one."

"Your brother could be furious."

Kelly shrugged. "It won't be the first time or the last. Brothers and sisters are always at each other's throats."

"He could be furious at me," Michael corrected.

"And that would be a first. I'm at a disadvantage, you know. Under normal conditions, I'd be a more than even match for him, but right now I'd prefer to pick fights I can win with words."

"So you'll smooth things over, if it comes to that," she said, clearly not taking his fears seriously. "It won't. I'm telling you, he's going to thank you. And I will certainly find some inventive way to demonstrate my gratitude."

Michael choked at the immediate image that slammed through him. "Inventive, huh?"

She grinned, clearly sensing victory. "Absolutely."

"Care to give me a small sample, just a little incentive offered in good faith?"

"Roll over," she ordered.

Michael cast one last, lingering look into her suddenly smoldering eyes and did as she'd asked. The sheet fell away. He wasn't entirely sure what he expected, maybe some new, exotically scented oil that would drive him wild. Maybe the light skim of her fingers just a little too high on the back of his thigh.

What he absolutely, positively had not expected was the light brush of her lips against the back of his calf, the back of his knee, the back of his thigh. If it hadn't been for one small, but very strong hand placed squarely in the small of his back, he would have jolted off the massage table and dragged Kelly straight into his arms and then onto his bed without giving propriety a second thought.

When she finally finished her little demonstration, his breathing was ragged and his resolve in tatters. He sighed heavily and tilted his head to meet her gaze.

"Bring me the phone."

She grinned, a cat content with its expected reward of cream.

"And don't look so damned smug," he added.

"Aye, aye, sir," she said cheerfully as she handed him the phone.

"I know I'm going to regret this," Michael muttered as he dialed Bryan's number.

Then he thought of the way Kelly's clever mouth had felt against his skin and concluded that even if her scheme blew up in their faces, he still might die a happy man.

Chapter Ten

Her brother truly was the biggest dolt on the planet, Kelly concluded as she watched him all but ignore Moira, who was seated next to him. And if sparks didn't start to fly soon, Michael was never going to let her forget it.

In fact, he chose that precise moment to lean in close and whisper, "It's going well, don't you think?" The edge of sarcasm in his voice was unmistakable.

"Well, do something," she snapped back.

His eyes widened. "Me? This was your idea."

"I'll make it worth your while," she offered.

He had the audacity to laugh at that. "Promises, promises."

One advantage of being with a man in a wheelchair was that his attention could be refocused in a heartbeat. Kelly snagged the handles on his chair and aimed him toward her brother and Moira. "Now, talk," she muttered.

The look Michael shot at her would have wilted the resolve of a lesser woman, but Kelly was feeling desperate. She wanted this evening to work out, not to guarantee Moira's silence—truthfully, that was a given anyway—but to try to ensure her happiness. If her friend was foolish enough to be interested in Bryan, then he was the man Kelly wanted for her. Not that she would ever have promoted such a scheme if she hadn't also believed that Moira was exactly right for her brother, she added piously.

"Great music," Michael ventured to Moira. "Are you enjoying it?"

Kelly had to fight a smile at his charming awkwardness. Clearly social graces had never been high on his list of achievements. She actually found that reassuring. She'd always assumed he'd been a rogue who flirted with anything in skirts, especially once he'd joined the navy. Handsome as he was, though, she doubted he'd needed much in the way of charm to have women circling around him.

When Moira remained absolutely silent, Kelly firmly poked an elbow in her ribs. "Michael asked you about the music."

Moira gave them both a weak smile. "Sorry. I guess I was thinking about something else. The music's very nice," she agreed politely.

"Are you very familiar with Irish music?" Michael asked, still doing his best to get the conversation rolling.

Kelly nearly groaned when her friend merely nodded. She knew for a fact that Moira loved Irish music and had been to a dozen or more pubs on a trip to

Ireland. She would have sworn this was the perfect topic to get her friend to be a little more animated and to catch Bryan's attention. He considered himself something of an expert on Irish folk tunes.

"You have been to Ireland, though," Kelly prodded. "How does this compare?"

Finally, Moira seemed to forget Bryan's apparently intimidating presence. Her expression brightened. "The lead singer's the best I've heard this side of Dublin," she said with her more familiar enthusiasm.

Bryan's attention was finally snagged. He regarded Moira intently. "You've been to Ireland?"

Moira blinked at him, clearly startled that he'd finally taken notice of her. "Well, of course," she said. "With a name like Brady, how could I not have gone at least once? Have you been?"

"Twice. Once on a tour by horseback. Another time hiking."

Moira's eyes lit up. "You actually went hiking? Where? Which tour company did you use?" The questions poured out of her. "I've been thinking of doing that next summer, but I can't decide which tour to take. Just when I think I've decided, I see another brochure that looks even better."

Kelly secretly congratulated herself on a job well done as the two of them put their heads together, shutting Michael completely out of the conversation. He turned back to Kelly slowly, his expression vaguely bewildered.

"What just happened there?"

"You asked the right question. I provided an extra push. And they took over from there." She patted his hand. "Nice work. You obviously have a knack for this sort of thing after all."

He frowned at that. "Don't go getting any ideas. This was a one-time thing, just to get you out of a bind." His gaze locked on hers. "Though I have the strangest feeling that your friend Moira was never any threat to your career in the first place. She doesn't seem the type to resort to blackmail to get a guy."

Kelly feigned surprise. "Really?" She shrugged. "Well, you never know. Better safe than sorry."

His gaze darkened as he subjected her to a thorough survey that had her skin heating.

"So, what do you think? Can we get out of here now?" he asked, his voice low and husky.

Something in his tone, in his eyes made her suddenly nervous. "And miss seeing the fruits of our labor? Why would we want to do that?"

He snagged her jacket off the back of her chair and tossed it to her. "Because we have better things to do," he said, already heading for the door.

Heat spiraled through her along with a little thrill of anticipation. "We do?" she asked, automatically trailing after him just as he'd obviously assumed she would.

"Remember all those inventive ideas of yours?" he said cheerfully. "It's time to pay up."

Her step faltered. "Now? Tonight?"

"Can you think of any reason to wait? A deal is a deal, right?"

"Well, sure, but tonight?" She glanced back to see that her brother and Moira still had their heads together. "What if they need us?"

"Their problem," Michael said succinctly. "We've done our good deed for the day, maybe for the year."

He leveled a look straight into Kelly's eyes that made her stomach flip over.

"Unless there's some reason you want to back out on our deal?" he suggested lightly.

Honestly, she had been sure that Michael would be the one backing out. After all, he was the one who'd listed all those reasons why they should keep their emotions in check and their hands to themselves. Her promise had been made half in jest, though with at least a modicum of wistful hope. Now that it appeared he was taking her up on it, she had to wonder if she'd made a mistake. As desperately as she wanted it, were they really ready to take this next step? Maybe they should think it over a little longer, weigh the pros and cons.

Was she crazy? This was exactly what she'd been wanting from the day she'd set eyes on him years ago. If they were finally on the same wavelength, why wait?

She held his gaze, her expression serious. "Lead on," she said quietly, accepting his challenge.

For an instant, Michael seemed startled by her acquiescence. Then he latched on to her hand and pulled her down until her face was even with his.

"Once we get in your car and head for my place, there's no turning back," he said tightly.

"We're not playing some silly game of chicken, Michael. I know that," she told him.

"Just so we're clear."

"Never more clear," she replied evenly. She was amazed at how cool she sounded, when her heart was hammering at least a hundred beats a minute. This was it, then, the night she'd been waiting for forever. And she was going to blow it by asking the one question guaranteed to bring on an attack of conscience in Michael.

"Why tonight?" she asked, studying his face intently.

His expression faltered ever so slightly. Most people wouldn't even have noticed, but Kelly did. She sighed heavily as regrets came crashing down around her.

"I thought so. No real reason, except that I offered you a deal, right?"

Now it was his turn to sigh. "That, and the fact that I'm an idiot. Scratch that. I'm a randy idiot. I want you, and you gave me the perfect excuse to take what I wanted."

"You still can," she said and meant it, even if the warm and fuzzy glow was fading rapidly.

He pressed her knuckles to his lips and kissed them. "Another time. Go back in there and keep an eye on your brother and your friend."

She knew it was the smart thing to do, the only thing, really. "How will you get home?"

He gestured toward the street where a taxi sat waiting, its motor running. "I already had Ryan call a cab for me. For a minute there, I was going to send it away, but saner minds prevailed."

Kelly stared at him incredulously. "You were testing me?"

"And myself," he said. "It was a stupid thing to do, and I apologize. At least we both learned a valuable lesson."

She wasn't much in the mood to view things in a particularly generous light. "Oh? What's that?"

"That it's increasingly likely that we're going to tempt fate once too often."

She frowned at him. "Don't be too sure of that,"

she said heatedly. "I think the lesson I learned is entirely different."

"Oh?"

"When it comes to playing games, you're a master, and that is definitely *not* a compliment."

That said, she whirled around and went back inside, leaving Michael to stare after her, his mouth open. Whatever words he'd been intending to say to try to pacify her this time, she hoped he choked on them.

Michael was getting exactly what he deserved, no question about it. Kelly's frosty attitude when she'd walked away on Friday night had lingered all through Saturday's therapy session and on into the couple of calls he'd made to try to apologize again for his inexcusable behavior. He'd taken something important and turned it into a contest to see which of them was stronger. He'd expected to be the winner by a mile, but he had to admit it had turned out to be a draw. Kelly was no slouch when it came to good sense and willpower.

Which left them exactly where? Truthfully, he was surprised she'd even shown up on Saturday, but clearly that powerful work ethic of hers had kicked in, along with a healthy dose of pride. It was evident, though, that the attraction between them could no longer be ignored.

The first time Michael had linked Kelly and hot, steamy sex in the same thought, he had cursed himself for an idiot. A few stolen kisses were one thing. They'd both been driven to distraction by circumstances, he had assured himself.

The second time his mind invented an image of the two of them naked in his bed, tangled together, he pictured just how many ways Bryan could devise to make him pay for taking advantage of his kid sister. That had temporarily put a damper on his desire to steal anything more than an occasional kiss.

Friday night he'd come too damned close to making those images a reality. He feared that the next time, his brain wouldn't kick in at all.

The only way to avoid temptation would be to fire her. Of course, that ignored the fact that she'd already quit...specifically so they could become more intimate, if they so chose. How was he supposed to fire someone who didn't technically work for him in the first place? And how could he explain it to her without making himself out to be even more of a jerk than she already thought him to be?

When Kelly's knock came promptly at 10:00 a.m. on Tuesday, he sucked in a deep breath and resolved to clear the air between them. He was halfway to the door when she used her key and came breezing in, a phony smile firmly in place. A desire to kiss her until that smile turned real slammed through him. That was not a particularly good sign.

"Good morning," he said, regarding her warily as he tried to gauge her real mood.

"Is it? I hadn't noticed." She flipped open her massage table and locked the legs into place. "Are you ready to get to work?"

Michael noted that the frost from Saturday had now turned to icicles. He had to hold back a sigh of regret.

"Sure," he said, climbing onto the table.

The first touch of her cold hands on his back was a shock. He noted that she hadn't bothered to warm the oil she was using today, or else it was simply no match for her body temperature or her mood.

"Starting Thursday, I think we should have our sessions at the rehab clinic," she informed him. "I've already spoken to Ryan and Maggie, and they'll be happy to drive you over there."

Something deep inside Michael turned hot and angry at her presumption. "What right did you have to go to my brother before coming to me?"

She didn't react to his tone. "I wanted to be sure transportation wouldn't be a problem. Since it isn't, I assume you have no objections to the change."

Michael moved away from her. "Are you scared, Kelly? Is that what this is about?"

"Don't be ridiculous," she snapped, her eyes flashing furiously. "You don't scare me. You're ready for equipment I can't haul around. You'll make faster progress if you have it. It's as simple as that."

"Then it's just a bonus for you that we won't be alone anymore?"

"Exactly," she said tightly.

Michael wanted to force her to admit that it wasn't his recovery, but her anger at him that was behind this sudden announcement. Instead, he put his head down without further comment, and let her continue with the massage.

He felt the brush of her breasts as she leaned closer to massage the tight, cramped muscle in his thigh. Instinctively, he glanced to his left and his gaze landed on her cleavage. Not that she was wearing anything the least bit revealing, just her usual V-neck T-shirt. It just so happened that it had dipped provocatively lower than normal. The sight of that smooth, pale skin snapped the last tiny hold he had on his restraint.

This time when he reached for her and closed his

mouth over hers, he knew things were going to be different. Unless she slapped him silly—which she probably should—he was going to do more than taste her lips. He was going to close his mouth over the pebbled tip of her breast. He was going to skim his tongue over that swell of satiny skin.

He was going to burn in hell.

He uttered a curse and pushed her away. She drew in a deep, raspy breath and stared at him.

''Why?'' she began in a choked voice.

''Why did I kiss you again? I think we both know the answer to that,'' he said wryly. He raked a hand through his hair. ''I swore I wasn't going to touch you, but you could tempt a saint. It's even worse when you get that chilly don't-touch-me note in your voice.''

A smile played at the corners of her mouth. ''Apparently you like a challenge.''

''What man doesn't?'' he said wryly. ''Can you imagine what would happen if you got it into your head to try to seduce me?''

''I…I couldn't,'' she stammered, looking shocked. ''I wouldn't.''

''But not because you don't want to,'' he said. ''Or because I don't want you to.''

''Because it's wrong,'' she said flatly. ''That was the conclusion you reached all on your own. On top of that, we've discussed this, Michael. We've gone over it every which way. I totally agree with you now that it's a bad idea.''

''I know,'' he soothed gently, even as he reached for her again and brushed his lips over hers. ''Are you absolutely sure that we ruled this out? I can't seem to remember anything except how much I want you.''

"When you do that, I can't remember anything, either," she admitted, then moaned as he claimed her mouth again.

Michael swore he was going to take only a quick taste of her minty sweetness, but it only made him crave more. "I'm sorry," he murmured against her lips. "Do you want me to stop?"

"Yes," she whispered, clearly dazed, then, "no."

His lips curved. "Which is it?"

"Oh, God, I wish I knew," she said, closing her mouth over his again.

Her kiss was hot and needy and sent desire ricocheting through him in a way he'd never expected to experience again. Her hands slid over his chest, the touch nothing like the professional strokes of her massages. This left a trail of wicked fire and yearning in its wake.

Michael found himself wanting to experience her pale, smooth skin in the same way. He tugged her T-shirt free from the waistband of her jeans and caressed the bare, hot flesh beneath. He stroked the curve of her breasts with his thumbs, then skimmed a finger across the already taut nipples. She jolted at the touch, then arched into it, a murmur of pleasure low in her throat. He flipped open the snap on her jeans and reached lower, dipping toward her moist, hot core.

"Come up here with me," he urged, wanting her on top of him, rubbing against the throbbing heat of his own arousal. Right? Wrong? He didn't care anymore. It was all about the sensation, the need that she stirred in him and the promise of pleasure that was just out of reach.

He had his hands around her waist and was about

to lift her when she seemed to snap out of the sensual daze she'd been in.

"No," she said shakily. "I need more than this from you. I deserve more than this."

Shaken by her words and by the suddenness with which she pulled away, he simply stared, breathing hard and trying to make sense of what had just happened. Given how many times he'd ended things before they got carried away, he supposed he had no right to complain, but he wasn't feeling especially rational at the moment, just needy.

"Was this some new therapy technique?" he inquired, hoping to lighten the charged atmosphere.

Something that looked an awful lot like hurt flashed in her eyes.

"Sure, that's exactly what it was," she said, the ice back in her voice. "Be sure to recommend me to your friends."

Before he knew it, she'd grabbed her purse and left without so much as a word of goodbye.

Michael stared after her, his heart thudding dully. "Well, you certainly blew that," he muttered. Driving her away was getting to be a habit, a truly lousy habit.

He spent a miserable two days worrying and wondering if she'd come back or if she'd send another therapist in her place. He should have realized that Kelly was made of sterner stuff. He'd certainly seen all the evidence of that.

Thursday morning at precisely 9:30, Maggie turned up. "Ready to go to the clinic?" she inquired cheerfully.

He had forgotten all about the damned clinic and Kelly's edict that further sessions would be conducted there with lots of witnesses around to prevent a repeat of their last couple of encounters. However, he was not about to let Maggie see his dismay. Heaven knew what she would make out of it.

"Let's go," he said grimly, reaching for his coat.

After they were in the car, his sister-in-law slanted a knowing look at him. "Anything wrong?"

"What could possibly be wrong?" he asked sourly.

"I thought maybe you were unhappy about no longer having Kelly to yourself for these sessions."

"Why would that bother me?"

She struggled with a grin. "No reason. You just seem a little off this morning."

"I've been a little off ever since I got shot," he retorted. "Or hadn't you noticed?"

"Well, of course, I have no way of knowing what your disposition was like prior to your getting shot, but you seem a little crankier than usual today, if you don't mind me saying so."

Michael sighed. "Would it stop you if I *did* mind?"

She laughed. "Not likely." Her gaze suddenly turned serious. "Why don't you just admit you're crazy about her? It would be a lot easier on everyone, you included."

"I can't be crazy about her," he said flatly.

"Why on earth not?"

He scowled at the question. "Do you even have to ask? She doesn't need an out-of-work man who can't even stand on his own two feet in her life."

Maggie shook her head. "There are so many things wrong with that statement, I hardly know where to begin."

"I don't suppose you could be persuaded to keep all of them to yourself?"

"Oh, please," she said, regarding him with disdain.

"First, if not having a job is an issue, get one. Ryan's friend is still anxious to talk to you. Second, you'll be back on your feet eventually, so that's a ridiculous excuse. And third, you need to stop feeling so blasted sorry for yourself and think about Kelly's feelings for a change. You're selling her short. You're assuming that she's some superficial twit who cares only about whether you have a good job or can run a marathon."

"I never said any such thing," he retorted indignantly.

"Maybe not in so many words, but the message is clear, just the same."

"It's not about her, it's about me," he said with frustration.

"Well, it's time to get over yourself, Devaney, and get on with the business of living."

"Have you ever considered a military career?" he inquired, more shaken by the scolding than he'd ever been by a dressing down from a superior officer in the navy.

"Nope. Couldn't take the discipline," she said at once.

"Then find some small country that needs a dictator. You'd be good at it."

She laughed. "If I get tired of running a pub with your brother, I'll keep that in mind. I'm not the one who's averse to considering other options," she said as she pulled to a stop in front of the clinic. "I'll get your wheelchair out of the back. Do you need help getting inside?"

He considered the doors and the challenge in Maggie's eyes. "I'll manage," he said tightly.

"Good answer," she said and gave his shoulder a reassuring squeeze.

Oddly enough, her approval made him feel marginally better as he went inside to face Kelly.

He spotted her at once, working with a young girl whose gait was awkward as she clung to two metal rails on either side of her. The girl couldn't have been more than sixteen and her brow was furrowed in concentration as she struggled to put one foot in front of the other and inch along between the bars. She hadn't gone more than a couple of feet, when Kelly beamed at her and patted her hand.

"Good work, Jennifer," she praised as she helped her into a wheelchair and took her over to a woman who'd been watching the scene with a shattered expression on her face.

Kelly smiled at the older woman. "Great progress today, don't you think?"

"Wonderful," the woman said, forcing a smile for the girl.

Jennifer searched the older woman's face as if she were looking for signs that she wasn't telling the truth, but the smile never wavered, and eventually Jennifer's lips curved into a half smile.

"I'm going to walk again, Mom. I really am," she said with gritty determination.

"Of course, you are," Kelly agreed. "I'll see you again on Saturday."

Shaken by the entire scene, Michael waited until they'd gone before joining Kelly.

"What happened to her?" he asked.

"Automobile accident," she said succinctly.

"How long ago?"

"About the same time as your injuries."

He caught the underlying message without her having to spell it out for him. Young Jennifer was braver and more determined than he was. In that instant, he knew what real shame felt like.

"Okay, then," he told her. "Let's get to work and get me up to speed." His gaze locked with hers. "After that we need to talk."

"No, we don't," she said emphatically.

Michael's leg might be all but useless, but his arms were as strong as ever. He latched on to her hand and tugged until she was standing right in front of him.

"Okay, then, we'll talk first. I'm sorry," he apologized.

She finally met his gaze. "For?"

"Making light of what happened between us the other day."

She shrugged. "It was a kiss. No big deal."

"It was more than a kiss and it was a big deal," he insisted. "I guess that's why I did it. I felt guilty for taking advantage of you."

"You?" she said incredulously. "I'm the one who took advantage. I'm the one who broke the rules."

He struggled with a grin. "You have rules about that kind of thing?"

"The two of us made rules about it."

"Then who better to break them?" he asked.

"We can't keep doing this," she said plaintively.

"It was a kiss," he said, echoing her words before adding, "A great kiss."

The beginnings of a smile tugged at her lips and she slanted a look at him. "Great, huh?"

He laughed at the hint of satisfaction in her voice. "Phenomenal."

"Okay, don't overdo it," she said. "I can live with great. Now, let's get to work."

"In a sec. There's one last thing I wanted to say."

"Oh?"

"I'm glad you haven't given up on me. It's more than I deserve."

She sighed. "There was never a question about that, Michael. I'm here for as long as you need me. There's nothing you could do that would chase me away."

The heartfelt commitment took him aback. Few people in his life had made that kind of commitment to him. His own parents certainly hadn't. The Havilceks had, but because adoption had been out of the question, there had never been that final leap to becoming a real family that he believed he could count on forever. The reservation had been his alone. He'd been scared to allow himself to feel too much for the Havilceks.

Beyond that, though he and Bryan had been as close as brothers, or at least as close as he'd remembered brothers being, they hadn't stayed in touch once he'd joined the navy.

Now here was a beautiful, compassionate, loving woman telling him she was in his life for as long as he needed her. An unfamiliar feeling filled his chest. He tried to pin a label on it, but couldn't.

Only later that night, when he was all alone in his cold bed, his leg throbbing, did it dawn on him what that feeling had been: contentment. If he could feel such a thing at the worst time of his life, then he owed the woman responsible. He owed her more than respect and fair play. He owed her his heart, and it was past time he proved he was capable of giving it.

Chapter Eleven

When there was a knock on Michael's door about six o'clock on Friday evening, he opened it, anticipating that he'd find Kelly on the other side. Instead, it was Sean, his usual jovial expression far more grim than Michael had ever seen it.

"Come on in. Is there a problem?" Michael asked his older brother.

"We need to talk," Sean said, looking around the apartment with a cursory glance.

Since it was the first time Sean had been to visit since Michael had returned to Boston, Michael assumed it had to be important, especially when they were supposed to see each other at the pub in less than an hour.

"Okay," Michael said cautiously, gesturing for him to come in. "I take it this is something we couldn't get into later at Ryan's Place."

"Too many people around," Sean said. "I figure you and I need to work this out and present a united front."

Michael sighed. "Then it's about the search for the rest of the family," he guessed.

Sean nodded. "You know where I stand on that. Where do you stand?"

Despite the conversation he'd had with his mother, since then Michael had tried to avoid giving the matter any serious thought at all. He'd been secretly hoping that Ryan would simply take the matter out of their hands and do whatever it was he felt the need to do.

"Have a seat," he said to Sean, just to buy himself some time to put his thoughts into words.

"I'll stand."

"And make me get a stiff neck trying to look you in the eye?" Michael inquired.

Sean immediately looked chagrined. "Sorry, man. I wasn't thinking." He sat down on the edge of the sofa. "Are you doing okay?"

Michael shrugged. "Kelly thinks I'm making progress."

"Well, she's the expert."

He thought of the young girl he'd seen at the clinic the day before and how guilty he'd felt when he'd seen how hard she was struggling to overcome her injuries. "Kelly's idea of progress and mine differ slightly, but that's going to change," he said with determination. He'd wallowed in self-pity and given lip service to his therapy long enough. Maybe he'd never be a SEAL again, but everyone had been right—there were plenty of things he could do. He just had to find the right one, something that challenged him mentally and physically. Captaining a charter boat might not be it, but there was something out there.

Sean regarded him with obvious discomfort. "I'm sorry I haven't been around much to help out. It's not that I didn't want to, it's just…"

Sean's voice trailed off, and Michael knew that his assessment of his brother's careful distance had been right on target. "It's just that my situation made you uncomfortable," he said. "I understand. I think when people like you and me, who work in a profession that requires top-notch fitness, run into a situation where someone's physically impaired, we see ourselves. The guys on my SEAL team were the same way when I was in the hospital in San Diego. They came around because they felt duty-bound to come, but they couldn't look me in the eye. It made all of us uncomfortable, me most of all."

Relief spread across Sean's face. "That's it exactly. It's sort of the there-but-for-the-grace-of-God-go-I thing. I got trapped in a fire last year trying to get my partner out. It turned out okay, but I think that brush with a potential tragedy put the fear of God in me. And now that I have Deanna and Kevin to consider…" He shrugged. "Maybe it's time to think about a new line of work."

"Would you be happy doing anything else?" Michael asked.

"Nothing I can think of," Sean admitted.

Michael sighed. "Same with me." He felt as if he and his brother were sharing a rare moment of being totally in sync, the way brothers ought to be. It was a strange—and oddly comforting—sensation.

"It doesn't do a damn bit of good to tell you it will all work out, does it?" Sean asked.

"Not much."

With nothing left to be said, Michael pushed the topic out of his mind. It wasn't a situation they could resolve today. Maybe they could figure out the pros and cons of this hunt for their parents and twin brothers, though.

"Sean, just how vehemently against this search are you?" he asked. "You've had longer to make peace with the idea than I have, yet you haven't done it."

"It's a funny thing about that," Sean said, looking pensive. "For years I waited for our folks to turn up to claim me. When I grew up and that hadn't happened, I told myself it didn't matter. In fact, I deliberately took pains to make it difficult for them to locate me—an unlisted phone number, no credit cards, the whole nine yards." He gave Michael a rueful look. "Ryan found me anyway."

"Which led you to believe that our parents never even tried," Michael concluded. That's the way he would have interpreted things, as well. And it would have hurt, if he'd allowed himself to dwell on it, just as it so clearly hurt his brother.

"They certainly didn't look hard enough, anyway." Sean's eyes were filled with bitterness and belligerence as he met Michael's gaze. "So, why should I care about finding them?"

"I can't argue with that," Michael said. "The way I see it, we don't owe them a damned thing, but maybe finding them is like finding a missing piece of a puzzle. You don't really care about it and it may not mean much in the grand scheme of things, but clicking that last piece into place can still complete things you'd never even realized you were wondering about. It can bring about a sense of closure where the past's concerned.''

Sean sighed heavily, clearly unhappy with Michael's assessment. "Then you're saying we should go to meet this Patrick.''

Michael nodded slowly as he reached his own decision. "Yeah, I think I am. I thought I had a lot to lose by looking for the rest of the family. I thought it would hurt the people who'd given me a home and raised me as if I were one of their own kids. But my mom made me see that I can never lose them, not really. I can only gain some answers, maybe even get my old family back.''

"You sure you want them?" Sean asked wryly.

Michael grinned. "Hey, if it goes badly, you, Ryan and I still have each other, which is more than we had before Ryan started looking. And it could go well. If that happens, well, a man can never have too many decent brothers watching his back, can he?" He regarded Sean intently. "But that's the way I see it. It doesn't mean you have to reach the same conclusion.''

"Yeah, right," Sean said. "But if I don't, the two of you will see me as holding out just out of pure stubbornness.''

"I won't," Michael reassured him. "It's your call, Sean. Seems to me like this is one of those times when the majority shouldn't necessarily rule. I don't know how Ryan will feel, but I say we need a unanimous vote to move on.''

Sean didn't look entirely convinced, but he finally sighed. "I'll go along with it," he said, not even trying to hide his reluctance. "I know Deanna thinks I should. And you and Ryan have given it a lot of thought. So what happens next?''

''If you're absolutely sure, then we'll tell Ryan tonight that the trip is on.''

''When do you want to go?''

Michael regarded his brother with an innocent expression. ''Just as soon as I'm out of this chair and can go on my own two feet.''

Sean reacted with surprise. ''After everything you just said, you want to wait?''

Michael chuckled. ''I said I wanted answers. I didn't say I was in a hurry to get them.''

Friday nights at Ryan's Place had turned into a regular thing, not only for the Devaneys, the O'Briens and the Havilceks, but for Kelly, Bryan and Moira. It had been two weeks since Kelly and Michael had set up her brother with her best friend, and the two had been pretty much inseparable since that awkward beginning.

Kelly glanced toward the tiny dance floor where Moira was attempting to teach Bryan an Irish jig. It wasn't going well. Kelly's brother had two left feet, which he kept tripping over. Moira was trying to hide her laughter, even as she patiently demonstrated the steps yet again.

Watching them instilled a feeling of melancholy in Kelly. Bryan and Moira hardly knew each other, but you could tell just looking at them that there was something special happening. She thought of her own situation with Michael and wondered if they would ever share that kind of closeness. They were totally in sync in so many ways and the chemistry was certainly powerful, but when it came to the important stuff, they kept bumping into roadblocks.

Even as the thought began to nag at her, she realized how contradictory it was, given the steamy kisses they'd shared. Yet something was missing in their relationship, something she could no longer deny. Sizzling attraction wasn't commitment, and that was what she wanted from Michael. She wanted forever, maybe not right now when he was still doing so much soul-searching about his own future, but at least the promise of forever once those questions were resolved.

"Hey, why the frown?" Michael asked, regarding her worriedly.

"Just thinking," she said evasively. This wasn't the time or the place to get into a discussion about their relationship. Maybe there was no appropriate time to get into it. Maybe she needed to accept that there would never be a relationship—at least not the kind she'd been hoping for—and move on with her life just the way she'd been encouraging Michael to do when it came to his career.

"It must be some pretty heavy thinking," he said, tracing his finger lightly over the furrow in her brow. "Anything I can help with?"

"No. It's under control." She forced a smile. "You said earlier that Sean came by. How was that?"

"Pretty great, actually. We really connected."

"I'm glad," she said with total sincerity. "It's wonderful that this whole reunion thing is working out so well for you."

He frowned. "Okay, that's it."

"What?" she said, startled by his reaction.

"You're suddenly being too blasted polite and—I don't know—distant, I guess. What's going on?"

"Nothing."

His scowl deepened. "So much for honesty and trust."

The jab hit home. Kelly sighed. "Okay, the truth is I was thinking about us, about how there really isn't an us, might never be an us, and I was trying to decide what to do about that."

"I see," he said slowly.

Since he looked more troubled than angered, she decided to press on. She regarded him earnestly. "I love being here with you, with your family," she told him honestly, "but it's an unhealthy situation for me."

He stared at her as if she'd suddenly started spouting Greek. "What the hell does that mean?"

"It means that I'm starting to care too much, not just about you, but about all of this," she said, gesturing around the table at the gathering of Devaneys, Havilceks and Maggie's relatives. "Right now, I'm your therapist. That's the only relationship that's real between us, the only one you're allowing to be real."

Michael looked genuinely bewildered by her claim. "Those kisses felt damn real to me."

She closed her eyes and tried to ignore the sensation of pure longing that suddenly swamped her. "I know," she said softly. "But they're not enough. Not anymore."

"What are you saying?"

She drew in a deep breath and faced him evenly. "I'm going to start seeing other people, and I won't be hanging out here anymore."

His expression turned hard. "Your choice."

A tide of hurt washed over her. If only he'd objected, fought even a little to change her mind, but he didn't. And that said everything. It said that whatever they had, he didn't think it was worth fighting for.

Kelly stood up, grabbed her coat and spun away from the table before anyone could see the tears that were starting to slide down her cheeks. As she raced for the door, she heard several people call her name, but she pretended she hadn't. She needed to be alone, needed to tell herself—probably a million and one times before she believed it—that she had done the right thing.

She was also going to need every single second between now and tomorrow morning to brace herself for having to face Michael at the rehab clinic, because even though it would be the smart, safe thing to do, she had no intention of abandoning him in the middle of his therapy.

Michael still wasn't entirely sure what the devil had happened the night before. One minute Kelly had been looking a little thoughtful, the next she'd been announcing that she was through with him. Maybe he was only a clueless male, but it didn't make any sense. He honestly had no idea what had triggered her announcement or her abrupt departure, not even after every single person in all of the combined families had tried to pry it out of him.

That had irritated him most of all, that Kelly had walked out, and he'd been left to answer an endless barrage of questions about what *he'd* done to make her go. Clearly everyone assumed that she couldn't possibly be the one at fault. He intended to have quite a lot to say about that when he saw her this morning at the clinic—*if* he saw her at the clinic.

He arrived with his heart admittedly in his throat as he scanned the mirrored therapy room for some sign of her. He spotted Jennifer, the teenaged patient who had inspired his own renewed dedication to his therapy, but she was working with someone else. His heart sank.

"Looking for Kelly?" Moira inquired, her tone every bit as cool as it had been the night before when she'd assumed that he had somehow driven Kelly from the pub.

He nodded.

"She's in a meeting with Dr. Burroughs. She should be free soon."

Michael couldn't describe the feeling of relief that spread through him. "Thanks." When Moira would have turned away, he caught her hand. "I didn't do anything to upset her last night. I swear it."

"If you say so."

"I do. I'm as confused as you are."

"If Bryan or I find out differently, there will be hell to pay," she said fiercely. "You know that, don't you?"

He had to admire that kind of loyalty, even if it did make him feel as if he'd been unwittingly targeted. "Everyone should have friends as protective as you are," he said. "I'll wait over there."

He felt Moira's gaze on his back as he wheeled himself across the room. He turned his back to the mirrored wall. He hated those mirrors. When he looked into them, he couldn't ignore his condition.

A few minutes later, he heard Kelly's laughter before he actually saw her. She emerged from an office with a man dressed in carefully creased slacks, a designer dress shirt and a lab coat. He was the epitome of everything Michael wasn't at the moment—suave, sure of himself and physically fit. Michael hated him on sight. Watching the way the man looked at Kelly set Michael's teeth on edge. If he'd been in any shape to do it, Michael would have slugged the man on the spot just as a matter of principle.

Even as the desire to punch the guy's lights out rocketed through him, he brought himself up short. He was jealous. He—a man who'd never had a jealous bone in his body—was feeling totally and thoroughly possessive about a woman he'd never even had a right to claim as his own. Well, hell. He was going to have to take a good long look at the reason for that, just not right now. Right now, he had to get across the room and protect his interests, even if he wasn't entirely sure why it mattered so much.

Kelly noticed him before her companion did. She frowned when she realized that he was heading straight for her, even though she was in the midst of a private conversation.

"Bill, I've got a client scheduled, and he's here now," she said. "I'll see you tonight at seven."

The doctor glanced in Michael's direction, gave him a distracted greeting, then turned his disgustingly toothy, white smile on Kelly. "I'll look forward to it."

"You didn't waste much time, did you?" Michael said sourly when Kelly finally turned to him.

"I beg your pardon?"

"Big date with the doc tonight, or did I misunderstand?"

"Whether I have a date with Dr. Burroughs tonight

or not is none of your business,'' she told him coldly. ''Are you ready to get to work today?''

He scowled at the dismissal of his question, but decided not to make an issue of it right now. First things first. He needed to get back on his feet, so he could show the doctor a thing or two about which of them was the better man.

By the time she got through the tense therapy session with Michael, Kelly's nerves were strained to the limit. It took everything in her not to go whining to Moira and ask that she recommend another therapist for him. The truth was, she didn't want to give up the time with him. And she wanted to be the one there with Michael when he walked on his own again.

She prayed that a hot shower and fifteen minutes of rest would improve her mood before her date. She had known Bill Burroughs for a couple of years now. He frequently referred his orthopedic patients to her when they needed rehab. He was attractive, intelligent and on his way to being filthy rich, even in today's fiscally tightfisted medical environment. He actually treated her as if she were a precious commodity. Most women would have been flattered, perhaps even charmed by his attentiveness and respect.

All Kelly could think about was the cantankerous man who'd kissed her till her toes curled, then apologized for making a joke out of it. Her teenage crush was turning into a full-blown case of grown-up lust, one she was determined to ignore if she and Michael were to go on working together. This date was supposed to help her accomplish that.

And it should have. It really should have. Bill pulled out all the stops. He took her to an elegant, romantic restaurant, ordered the finest champagne, told her how beautiful she looked.

When the orchestra played, he held her in his arms as if she were more fragile than spun glass and more valuable than diamonds. She gazed up into his dark brown eyes and wished they were other eyes, crystal-blue eyes.

"You seem distracted," Bill said. "Worried about one of your patients?"

"In a way," she said, hoping he'd let the subject drop.

He gave her one of his brilliant smiles, but suddenly it seemed practiced and artificial, not like the blinding sunlight of one of Michael's rare smiles.

"Do you want to talk about it? Maybe I can help."

And he would, too. Bill was always generous with his time, always willing to offer treatment suggestions whenever she had doubts about the appropriate course for a particular patient. Now, though, she shook her head. "Thanks, that's okay."

He led the way back to their table, then studied her for a long time. "You need a break, Kelly. You've been working too hard."

"No time," she said.

"Make time," he said firmly. "If there's one thing I've had to learn, it's that too much work winds up being counterproductive. You end up making bad decisions when you're under stress."

She heard what he was saying and knew he was right. Maybe she could use a break, even a week away might bring some perspective to the whole situation. And a week off from his therapy wouldn't set Michael back that much, or if he insisted, Moira or someone else could fill in.

"I'll think about it," she promised Bill.

His gaze warmed. "Don't think. Go with the flow. I could take a few days off and we could go someplace with warm beaches and tropical drinks. How does that sound?"

It was twenty degrees outside and snow was threatening. How did he think it sounded? If Michael had asked, she'd have been packing. As it was, she simply stared at Bill in shock. "You want me to go away with you?"

"Why not? It doesn't have to be a big deal."

Memories of Phil's sleazy proposition rang in her head. Was she the kind of woman men expected to be easy? Why the heck was Michael the only one who ever showed any restraint around her?

She met Bill's expectant gaze. "Call me old-fashioned, but to me it does sound like a big deal. We hardly know each other."

"Then what better way to get to know each other than a few uninterrupted days together in some romantic setting?" he asked, clearly confident that he could overcome her objections.

"Sorry, I can't," she said flatly.

Unlike Phil, Bill took her refusal with a smile. "No problem," he said, as easygoing as ever. "Let me know if you change your mind."

She didn't say it, but if tonight had proved nothing else, it was that she wasn't even the tiniest bit interested in Bill Burroughs, despite all the superficial things they had in common. In fact, she had pretty much spent the entire evening feeling like a fraud.

Minutes later, she told him she thought it was time to be going. He accepted that, as well.

When he walked her to her door, she let him kiss

her, hoping that it would banish the memory of another kiss. Instead, it was a tepid reminder that real passion required more than simply locking lips.

"Thanks, Bill. I had a lovely time," she said politely.

"So did I. We'll do it again soon," Bill said.

Kelly shook her head. "I'm sorry, Bill. You're a great guy, but…" Her words faltered.

Bill regarded her knowingly. "But your heart belongs to somebody else. I spent this whole evening hoping I was wrong about that. But it's the man I met at the clinic this morning, isn't it? I could sense that there was more going on there. He looked as if he'd like to beat me to a pulp for talking to you."

She regarded him with surprise. She hadn't expected him to see her feelings so clearly when she was still grappling with the truth herself. As for his assessment of Michael's feelings, she'd missed that completely.

"You're an intuitive man. My heart does belong to someone else." She saw no need to confirm that it was Michael. "I think it always has. I'm sorry for wasting your time. You planned such a lovely evening. I didn't deserve it."

Bill leaned down and pressed a chaste kiss to her cheek. "Nonsense. Don't be sorry. Spending an evening with you could never be a waste of time. Whoever he is, he's a lucky guy. And if things don't work out, give me a call. I'd like another chance. That tropical beach will still be there."

After she'd gone inside and settled into a warm bath filled with fragrant bubbles, Kelly allowed herself to think about Bill's words. She wondered if Michael would consider himself lucky if he knew how she felt.

As hard as she was trying—as hard as they both were working—she could never give him the one thing he clearly wanted. Oh, she would get him walking again. No question about that, given the progress they were already making.

But, even though they mostly avoided the subject, they both knew his career with the SEALs was over and he was a long way from making peace with that. She couldn't help thinking that he'd consider her love to be little more than second prize.

Chapter Twelve

Saturday had been the longest damn night of Michael's life. He'd refused several offers of company and spent the entire evening brooding over what Kelly and her date might be up to. The mere fact that she even *had* a date was annoying. Granted, things between the two of them were a little uncertain, but all that heat had to mean something. How could he have misread the signals between them so badly? Why the hell had she felt the need to take off with that pretty-boy doctor? What did he have to offer that Michael didn't, besides a body on which all the parts presumably worked?

Just thinking about what the two of them could be up to soured his mood. His bad temper didn't improve on Sunday or Monday. In fact, by the time he got to the rehab center on Tuesday morning, he was half out of his mind with imagining the worst—that she'd

gone and fallen head over heels in love with that annoying, expensively dressed jerk of a doctor. He
wasn't prepared to examine why that seemed to matter
so blasted much to him.

As Kelly approached him, Michael studied her face,
looking for evidence that something had changed. She
looked a little wary, a little pensive, but other than
that, he couldn't read anything into her expression.
When she finally met his gaze, she managed to muster
an unenthusiastic smile, then went into what he'd
come to recognize as her crisp, no-nonsense professional mode.

"I thought we'd try getting you out of that chair
today," she chirped cheerfully. "Are you game?"

Michael debated calling her on the phony attitude,
but her plan for the day caught his attention. "I've
been getting out of the chair," he pointed out.

She gestured toward the parallel bars where he'd
first seen Jennifer struggling to walk. Hope—along
with something that felt a whole lot like panic—swept
through him.

"You want me to walk?" he asked incredulously.

She did smile at that. "Hasn't that been the idea
all along? I thought you were chomping at the bit to
get back on your feet. I think you're strong enough
now. Your arm and shoulder muscles were already in
great shape. The weight work has strengthened your
leg muscles the last couple of weeks. It's time to start
standing on your own two feet again, Michael. I'm
not expecting you to run a marathon. Standing up for
a few minutes to put some real weight on that leg will
be good enough."

"But…" The protest died on his lips. This was

what he wanted, maybe too much. What if he stood up and fell flat on his face?

"You're not going to fall," Kelly reassured him, as if he'd voiced the fear aloud. "You'll have the bars to hold on to and I'll be there."

Falling into her arms was not an option. He'd never survive the humiliation of it. He weighed that against the cowardice implied by not trying at all. It was no contest. He had to do this, and maybe it was better that she'd taken him totally by surprise. He hadn't had to spend the whole weekend worrying about it.

Totally focused now, he met her gaze evenly and gave her a curt nod. "Let's do it."

She guided his chair to the bars, then placed herself between them and in front of him. "Want some help getting out of the chair?"

"No," he said tersely. If he was going to do this, he was going to do it on his own. He needed to learn to rely on himself again, the way he once had without giving it a second thought.

Kelly shrugged off his tone and gestured for him to get up on his own.

Michael set the brake on the chair, then reached for the bars and pulled himself up, grateful for the years of SEAL training that had, indeed, kept his shoulders and arms powerful. But once he was upright between the bars, his legs felt as wobbly as a newborn's, despite all the work they'd been doing to strengthen the muscles.

"Just take a minute and steady yourself," Kelly said quietly. "Remember this isn't some sort of test on which you're going to be graded. A step or two will be enough. Let's see how that injured leg takes to having some weight put on it."

Michael held himself upright by sheer will, terrified to put any weight at all on his bum leg. What if the surgeries and the pins weren't going to be enough, after all? What if the bones hadn't healed sufficiently? What if he crumpled to the floor right here? He could tolerate whatever pain there might be, but not the disappointment of failing, especially in front of Kelly.

But what if he didn't fail at all? He clung to that thought as he sucked in a deep breath and put his foot down gingerly. Slowly he began to put a little weight on it. To his relief, nothing immediately snapped in two. His bones and the various pieces of hardware the doctors had installed were apparently strong enough to keep him upright, at least. He added a little more weight until he was evenly balanced on both feet. It was an odd sensation, scary and exhilarating at the same time. Who would have thought that just standing up would give him such a sense of accomplishment, after the thousands of far more strenuous exertions to which he'd subjected his body?

Standing there, clinging to the bars with a white-knuckled grip, he ventured a glance at Kelly. Seeing her from this perspective—the way a man ought to be able to look a woman straight in the eye—made him want to drag her straight into his arms, but he forced the wistful thought aside.

"Looking good," Kelly said, giving him an encouraging smile. She backed up a step. "Now come here."

He met her gaze. "What's the incentive?" he asked, a deliberate dare in his voice.

One brow arched. "Walking again's not enough?" she asked.

"I was thinking such a momentous stride forward in our therapy ought to at least net me a kiss."

She frowned at that. "Take the step, then we'll talk about it."

"A peck on the cheek, then," he coaxed, enjoying the patches of color blooming on her face. He studied her with a considering look. "What's the harm, unless you and the good doctor are now an item?"

Her cheeks paled. "Leave Dr. Burroughs out of this."

Michael promptly took heart. "Bad date?" he inquired sympathetically. "I could have told you that. The guy is obviously too self-absorbed to be good company."

Kelly scowled at him. "I don't know how you came up with that," she snapped. "He was very good company. And why are we talking about him at all? You're supposed to be concentrating on taking that first step."

"Frankly, right this second, I'm finding this conversation a whole lot more fascinating," he said. "Something tells me you didn't have a good time."

"And you find that something to gloat about?"

"No, I merely find it interesting. Tell me, how did it go?"

Her scowl deepened. "Why are you pushing this? My date is none of your business."

"That's not the way I see it," Michael told her.

She gave him an impatient look. "I do."

"Come on, Kelly. I think I have a right to know if the woman who's been willing to risk her professional reputation to kiss me has found some other man she'd prefer to spend her free time with." He gave her a considering look. "Well, have you? Are you planning on spending more evenings with the preppy doctor?"

"If you must know, the answer is no. I won't be seeing Dr. Burroughs again."

He grinned, not even trying to hide his relief. "Glad to hear it. Does that mean I get my kiss?"

Suddenly the ice in her eyes seemed to melt. She gave him one of her more irrepressible grins. "If you can catch me," she said, backing up another step, then one more for good measure.

Michael's grin spread. "Sweetheart, don't you know you should never dare a SEAL?" If it took every last ounce of strength he possessed, he was going to meet her challenge. He'd been obsessing about kissing her all night long. He wasn't about to lose his chance now.

The first step was awkward and painful. It was impossible to imagine that walking, running and mountain-climbing had once been second nature to him. Sweat beaded on his brow and the muscles in his arms quivered with the tension of holding himself upright.

Thank God, he had long legs. He could reach her in one more stride. He took that step thanks to sheer grit and determination. As he steadied himself, he closed one hand over hers where it rested on the bar and gazed deep into her eyes.

"Pay up," he said softly.

There was no mistaking the heat that flared in her eyes as she lifted herself on tiptoe and brushed a quick, disappointing kiss across his lips.

"Oh, no, you don't," he whispered against her mouth, leaning heavily against one bar, while he slipped an arm around her waist and held her tight.

"I caught you fair and square. Now, pay up with a kiss that means something."

He heard her breath hitch, felt the heat radiating from her as she sighed and leaned into him, her breasts soft against his chest, her lips parted under his.

"Better," he murmured, as he plunged his tongue deep inside to taste her…to claim her.

When they were both breathing hard, he released her, then realized that the kiss had drained him of every last ounce of strength. Cursing his weakness, he struggled to turn himself around and make his way back to his wheelchair, angrily brushing off Kelly's offers of assistance.

Only after he was safely seated again did he allow himself to meet her gaze. To his amazement, she was grinning broadly.

"What?" he growled, feeling like a toddler who'd taken his first brave step, only to land solidly on his backside.

She regarded him as if he were crazy to have to ask. "You walked, Michael! You did it!"

As the enormity of that sank in, his irritation faded and a grin began to spread across his face. "By God, I did, didn't I?" He'd felt less triumphant after surviving a dangerous mission. He met Kelly's gaze. "If I could dance you around the room, I would."

"I'll hold you to that," she said. "Something tells me it won't be long."

Meeting her gaze, wanting her, Michael knew that no matter when it happened, it wouldn't be nearly soon enough.

Those first couple of faltering steps could be either the beginning of something or the end, Michael concluded when he had time to himself later that night. In a few weeks, Kelly would start cutting back on his therapy, leaving him to his own devices while she moved on to use her considerable skill with another patient who needed her more. As badly as he wanted to feel whole and able-bodied again, the prospect of losing Kelly forever was out of the question. He didn't know why he was so sure of that, but he was.

Whatever the pace of his recovery from here on out, he was going to have to make damn sure that Kelly stayed in his life, at least until he could figure out the hold she seemed to have over him. There would be no more little adventures for her with the Dr. Burroughses of the world. He wanted to be the one who occupied her thoughts and her time.

For a man who'd spent much of his life being totally driven and goal-oriented, this was just one more challenge to be met. Like any SEAL mission he'd ever planned and executed, it was a matter of logistics and precision. He intended to start with his Thursday therapy session, since that was the one time he could be guaranteed that she wouldn't bail on him. He was going to dazzle her with his progress, then set out to capture her heart.

For the forty-eight hours between sessions, he practiced standing until he could remain upright and steady without grabbing on to the nearest stable object to break an impending fall. By the time night came, his muscles ached from the strain and his leg was giving him fits, but it was a small price to pay.

On Thursday he wheeled himself into the rehab center with a renewed sense of confidence and purpose. Kelly seemed to sense the change in attitude, because she studied him with a quizzical expression as he hefted himself out of the chair and onto the parallel bars without being asked.

"I gather you're ready to start," she said, a spark of amusement in her eyes.

"I am," he said firmly. "Back up."

She hesitated. "I think it's better if I stay here."

He scowled until she finally shrugged and backed away, leaving nothing to impede him should he actually be able to manage to walk the entire length of the parallel bars. Gritting his teeth, Michael took the first step. It was actually easier than it had been at his apartment without any solid support to cling to. His confidence grew with the second step and then the third.

"Michael, don't push too hard," Kelly warned as he kept coming. "You don't want another injury now."

"I'm not going to fall," he insisted, his voice tight as he tried to gauge the remaining steps. Four, maybe. Three, if he could lengthen his stride to something better than these shuffling half steps. He sighed. Maybe he'd better settle for baby steps, as exasperating as that was. It was better than falling flat on his butt at her feet.

He noted that despite her warning, she hadn't rushed forward to cut him off, but she was holding her breath.

"You know, if you don't let out that breath you're holding, you're going to turn blue," he admonished lightly.

She sighed. "Sorry. I'm just afraid you're moving too fast."

He snorted at that. "I've seen snails move faster."

"You know what I mean, Michael."

All the while they bickered over whether or not he was overexerting himself, he kept moving forward with his awkward, shuffling gait. And then he was there, toe-to-toe with her, close enough to see the spark of admiration in her eyes, despite the admonitions tripping from her lips.

His legs were protesting the strain he'd put on them. His powerful arms were the only things keeping him upright, which meant he had to get through this next part in a hurry. Still standing, he met her gaze.

"Have dinner with me tomorrow night," he suggested.

She blinked rapidly. "What?"

"It's not a difficult concept. I asked you to have dinner with me."

"Why?"

He grinned at her reaction. "The usual reasons. Man meets woman. Man is attracted to woman. He asks her on a date. That is how it goes, isn't it? I'm not that much out of touch." He shrugged, trying not to make too much out of it. "Besides, I think we're past due for a celebration. You certainly deserve one for putting up with me all this time."

"Tomorrow's Friday," she pointed out.

Michael grinned. "I know that."

"You usually go to the pub on Fridays, and I told you how I feel about going there."

"You don't want to give my family any ideas about the two of us," he recited. "I know that, too. This is a date, Kelly. I'm asking you out on an honest-to-goodness date. No pub. No family. Just the two of us. You'll have to drive, but other than that I'm in charge for a change. We'll go wherever you want. Someplace fancy with candlelight and good wine. I'm afraid dancing's out, but who knows, maybe I'll buy you a corsage.''

She laughed then. ''Nobody buys corsages except for proms.''

''Too much?''

''Definitely.''

''Champagne, then. What do you say?''

She took so long answering that he thought she might actually turn him down, but finally she nodded. ''I would love to go to dinner with you, Michael. What time should I pick you up?''

''Seven sound okay?''

''Perfect,'' she agreed more eagerly. ''I'll pick the place and make a reservation.''

He shook his head. ''Tell me. I'll call. I need to remember how it's done.''

''I think it will all come back to you fairly quickly,'' she said wryly.

Her belief that he'd been a bit of a scoundrel was very flattering, but the truth had been something else entirely. Before joining the navy, he hadn't wanted to get distracted by a woman. During his years as a SEAL, the unpredictability of his life had kept him from getting too close. His relationships had been hot and steamy for a time, but there wasn't one he could look back on as being remotely meaningful.

''This is different,'' he told her with total sincerity.

''How? Because it's been so long?''

''No.'' He met her gaze and felt the familiar thunder of his pounding heart. ''Because it's you.''

Because it's you. Because it's you.

Kelly couldn't seem to stop Michael's words from echoing through her head. What had he meant? It had almost sounded as if he was genuinely worried about getting it right because she mattered to him in some way all the other women had not.

"Don't be ridiculous," she muttered as she tossed aside what had to be the tenth outfit she'd tried on. She had deliberately picked an informal restaurant, despite Michael's offer of champagne. He was still taking occasional pain medications and had no business drinking more than the occasional beer he indulged in with his pizza at home. Besides, her wardrobe was far more suited to casual than fancy.

Even so, she couldn't seem to find a blasted thing in her closet that satisfied her. She finally settled for a sage-green cotton sweater that somehow made her gray eyes seem more the soft green of jade. She added a pair of camel-colored wool slacks and a gold locket that her mother had given her for her thirteenth birthday. Inside, still, was a tiny picture of Michael she'd clipped from a snapshot that had been taken of him and Bryan on a trip to Cape Cod that summer. She'd kept that locket in her jewelry box for years, but something told her tonight was a perfect night to bring it out again. Of course, if he happened to ask what was inside, she'd probably die of embarrassment.

Michael's exuberant mood from Thursday afternoon had faded by the time she arrived to pick him up. His face was tight with pain. She took one look at him, assessed that he was paying for having overdone it the day before, and firmly closed the door behind her.

"Did you take your pain medication?" she asked as she moved briskly past him and headed for the kitchen where he kept the pills.

He shook his head.

She whirled on him. "Dammit, Michael, that's what the medication's for."

"Who said I was in pain?" he snapped.

The man's determination to be a stoic no matter the cost exasperated her beyond belief. She regarded him with amusement. "Are you saying you're not?"

"No more than usual," he insisted.

"Okay, then, get on your feet and let's get out of here."

The withering look he shot her would have terrified most people. Kelly simply stood there and waited.

"Okay, dammit, get the pill," he said, his voice tight with fury. "Just one."

She brought back the pill and a glass of water. "Why don't I fix dinner right here?"

He shook his head. "Absolutely not. I promised you a celebration."

"Michael, we can celebrate right here. It's private. The refrigerator's well stocked. I can whip something up in no time."

"It doesn't seem like much of a date."

"It works for me."

His gaze searched hers. "You really wouldn't mind?"

"Being alone with you? Hardly," she said lightly, then fled to the kitchen before he could react.

She heard the whispered glide of his wheelchair as she was pulling dishes from the cabinet, then the locking sound of the brake. When she finally turned around, Michael was struggling to his feet.

"What are you doing?" she demanded, starting forward.

"Stay where you are," he commanded.

"But—"

"Just this once, do what I ask," he said, slowly walking toward her. "And set those dishes down."

She regarded him with confusion. "Why?"

"Because if I do this right, you'll just wind up dropping them," he said, his expression solemn.

Filled with a sudden rush of anticipation, Kelly set the dishes down with a thump just before Michael drew her into his arms. He tucked a finger under her chin, searched her face intently, then lowered his mouth to cover hers.

Tenderness exploded into urgent need. Years of pent-up longing gave way to the thrill of satisfaction as Michael's kiss turned dark and dangerous. This was the way a man kissed a woman he wanted, Kelly thought as her senses went spinning.

"I want you," he murmured against her lips. "I'd intended to do this right. A little wining and dining the way you deserve, then trying to coax you back here and into my bed. If it's a lousy idea, tell me now."

Kelly could barely breathe, barely think, her heart was pounding so hard. "It's the best idea you've had in years," she said with conviction.

"Dinner?"

"I'll turn off the oven." She met his gaze. "Condoms?"

He grinned at that. "In the nightstand."

"Which means we have to get to your bedroom," she said.

For an instant, he looked uneasy. "The gallant thing would be to carry you," he said.

She glanced toward the wheelchair. "I could always ride in your lap."

For an instant, she thought he might refuse her out

of stubborn pride, but then apparently the possibilities began to intrigue him. He sat and she settled into place, wriggling a bit in the process.

"Watch it," he warned.

She regarded him with deliberate innocence. "Am I bothering you?"

"Sweetheart, you've been bothering me since the first day you walked through my front door all full of sass and determination."

"Is that so?" she asked, pleased. "Then your patience is amazing."

"I thought so."

The trip to the bedroom took a whole lot longer than it needed to, simply because Kelly did her best to bother him along the way.

"Game's over," he said when they were beside the bed.

Kelly met his gaze, let the heat between them build to a slow simmer, then shook her head. "No, Michael. It's just beginning."

Chapter Thirteen

Over recent months, Kelly thought she'd learned just about everything there was to know about Michael's body. After all, she'd massaged him, she'd seen his undeniable reaction to her touches. She knew the power of his shoulders and arms, the slowly fading scars on his legs, the less visible scars from old injuries he'd refused to discuss. But all of that had been different. She'd forced herself to hold back, to try not to react to him as a woman. She'd been at least moderately successful.

Now, however, she was able to give free rein to her curiosity, to caress his hard muscles and explore his body far more intimately than prior prudence had allowed.

In the bedroom, he shifted from the wheelchair to the edge of the bed. Kelly knelt beside him and tugged his dress shirt free from his slacks. For the first time, she realized how much care he'd taken with his appearance tonight.

"It's almost a shame to get you out of this," she said, even as she began undoing the buttons. "You look incredibly handsome. The blue matches your eyes."

"Is that so?" he said, as if it were a surprise and of little consequence. Instead, his intense gaze seemed to find the quick work she was making of his buttons fascinating. "You're awfully good at that."

"What, this?" she asked innocently, as she slowly spread the flaps of his shirt apart, then helped him shrug out of it. Then she slipped her fingers under the edge of his white T-shirt, her knuckles grazing warm, supple skin. She took her time lifting the soft cotton shirt higher and higher, allowing herself the titillating pleasure of a slow, deliberate revelation of his bare chest with its swirls of dark, crisp hair.

Tossing aside the T-shirt with its fresh laundry scent, she bent to press a kiss to his skin. The heat seemed to come off of him in waves. She was half-surprised it didn't sear her lips. As if it might, she kept her mouth moving, tasting him, peppering little kisses across his shoulders and the base of his throat. She could hear the hitch in his breath, feel the pounding of his heart under her palm. Knowing that she could make Michael respond to her was amazing. She had never felt more desirable in her entire life.

Still contemplating the wonder of his reaction, she gasped when his arm suddenly circled her waist and he lifted her around to stand between his legs.

"My turn," he announced, his gaze hot as he lifted the soft green sweater over her head. The action tousled her hair, but he reached up with total concentration and gently smoothed it back into place, his touch lingering on her cheeks.

"You're so soft," he whispered, his voice husky and filled with something that might have been awe.

What could have been an agony of indecision raced across his face, before he met her gaze. "This could be a bad idea."

Kelly immediately guessed his concern. Touched that he had let his need for her supercede his vulnerability, she reached for him, feeling the hard press of his arousal through his slacks.

"It doesn't seem like such a bad idea to me," she reassured him.

"I'm not exactly agile," he said, sounding suddenly angry and defensive, reactions more in keeping with a man who was putting his masculinity to the ultimate test, rather than an injured leg that had affected only his mobility.

She grinned and smoothed away the furrow in his brow. "But I am," she said. "Lay back and enjoy it, Devaney. Everything works that needs to work."

Heat and yearning glinted in his eyes. "You surprise me."

"Glad to hear it," she said, already fumbling for the buckle of his belt.

Michael covered her hands and stilled them. "Slow down. There are a few things I know I can still do," he said, regarding her with renewed eagerness. "Then you can take over."

Swift, sure hands swept over her breasts, releasing the front hook on her bra in the blink of an eye. Michael smoothed away the scraps of lace, his smoldering gaze steady as he surveyed her.

"You are so gorgeous," he whispered, his voice

satisfyingly husky. A wry grin tugged at his lips. "And I keep waiting for your brother to come charging in here to smash my face in."

Kelly chuckled. "Not an image to dwell on. Besides," she reassured him, "I have it on very good authority that his time is otherwise occupied tonight."

"Moira?"

"Moira. They're a hot item, thanks to us."

Michael grinned. "Well, good for us," he said, then closed his mouth over the tip of her breast.

The action sent a jolt of fire straight through her. Conversation died, lost to a rising tide of sensation that threatened to pull Kelly under, gasping for breath and clinging to Michael like a lifeline.

He might claim not to be agile, but he had more than enough moves to sweep her off her feet and onto a roller-coaster ride that left her feeling exhilarated and needy as they raced for the precipice and then, finally, at long last plunged over the edge in a giddy, amazing descent that had her screaming out with the wonder of it.

This was what she'd waited for her whole life, Kelly thought as the satisfying shudders slowly faded and contentment settled in. This was what sex was meant to be when two people really, truly connected on every conceivable level. This was what people meant when they talked about sex being transformed into making love.

And now that she'd discovered it, there was no way in hell she would ever let it go.

Michael woke up sometime later feeling astonishingly rested and satisfied in the way a man only felt after rambunctious, steamy sex. Okay, it hadn't been all that rambunctious, but it had been a helluva ride. And Kelly had ridden him over the brink, astonishing him with her abandon.

Discovering that he was still able to please a woman in bed did more for Michael's recovery than all the other therapy Kelly had provided. He'd needed not just the physical release, but the reassurance that his diminished agility hadn't really reduced him to a shell of the man he'd once been, at least not in one important facet of his life. He'd known all along that his assumptions about himself were exaggerated and based on fear, not common sense, but until now he hadn't been able to let go of them. Now, he thought, he was finally ready to move on, put his weaknesses into perspective and work to overcome them.

So what if he couldn't scramble up the side of an enemy ship with the quickness of a cat? So what if he'd never again run at a sprinter's pace? In time he would eventually be able to do most physical activities at a level equal to that of many civilians. And even now, when his first steps were still awkward and tortured, he'd been able to do the horizontal mambo in a more than satisfactory manner. If he could bring pleasure to Kelly—and himself—then complaining about the rest seemed pointless.

He had pleased her, too. There was no mistaking the flare of heat in her eyes, the soft moans of pleasure, the quick, urgent thrusts of her hips as they'd climbed higher and higher before tumbling together into a stormy sea of sensations.

He'd also read something else in her eyes, something he wasn't entirely sure how to interpret, something that terrified him. While he'd been selfishly grabbing at the one act guaranteed to reassure him that he was still a man, he suspected Kelly had been turning her long-ago crush into a full-fledged love affair. Though what had just happened between them had been incredible—inevitable, even—he wasn't quite ready to pin a label on it. He certainly wasn't ready to build a future around it.

Okay, maybe he was jumping the gun. Maybe Kelly was no more anxious for marriage and commitment than he was. Maybe she was perfectly capable of handling a torrid affair that stemmed from all the restless heat simmering between them for weeks now.

He glanced over at her tousled hair, her rosy cheeks and innocent expression and muttered a curse under his breath. No way was this woman ready for a torrid, meaningless affair. No way did she deserve anything less than happily-ever-after. And deep down, in a place he'd been trying to avoid examining too closely, he wanted to give her that. He just wasn't sure he could, not until he had answers to all the questions still burning in his gut.

Beyond passion and the promise of a pension from the navy, what did he really have to offer her? He was still only a shadow of his former self. Oh, he would be back on his feet, capable of walking more than a few feet, in a matter of weeks now, but what the devil was he going to do with himself then? More than most, he knew the value of having a profession that mattered, not for the money, but for the self-respect, something that despite the Havilceks' best efforts had eluded him until he'd become a SEAL. How was he going to find that self-respect again in his altered world?

Up until now he'd been consumed with proving the doctors wrong and walking again. Now he was going to have to face the fact that the fight ahead to find a new role for himself was going to be just as challenging. And, unfortunately, this was one challenge Kelly couldn't help him meet. He was going to have to face it squarely on his own.

He glanced down at her as she sighed and snuggled more tightly against him. At least now, though, he had a reason outside of his own ego to make something of his life. He'd desperately needed that motivating factor, probably in a way that wasn't entirely smart or healthy. Bottom line, though, Kelly had given him a reason to move on.

As if she sensed his turmoil, Kelly turned restless, then slowly stretched and blinked before finally focusing on his face.

"Hi," she murmured, reaching for the sheet as if she'd suddenly turned shy.

Michael kept the sheet just out of reach. "Don't," he chided. "I like looking at you."

She seemed startled by that. "You do?"

He grinned. "Come on now. You're a gorgeous woman. I'm a red-blooded male. Who knows what looking might lead to."

Her eyes sparkled with sudden fascination. "Really? Tell me."

"Why don't I show you?" he said, reaching for her. It took him over an hour to make his point to his thorough and complete satisfaction. Kelly gave herself up completely to him, holding nothing back. She was remarkable.

For Michael, the effort proved one thing beyond a

shadow of a doubt. He had to be able to come to her as the kind of man she deserved...or he had to let her go.

Kelly knew she was probably behaving like a giddy schoolgirl when she arrived at the rehab clinic early Saturday morning for her weekly coffee and sugar-laden treats date with Moira, but she couldn't help it. Last night had been the most magical night of her life. If it showed on her face, if she couldn't seem to stop smiling, well, too bad. Moira was the one person she could count on to understand completely. She'd been grinning a lot lately, too.

Kelly walked into her boss's office and plunked the bag of doughnuts on Moira's desk, then handed her the paper cup of latte from the trendy coffee shop down the street. Moira glanced up from her pile of paperwork, tossed down her pen and studied Kelly's face with searing intensity.

"Uh-oh," she said eventually. "Something happened between you and Michael, didn't it?"

"Did I ask you to tell all when you and Bryan got together?" Kelly inquired airily.

"You didn't have to ask," Moira pointed out. "I babbled like an infatuated idiot. You owe me the same courtesy."

"You'll just tell me what a mistake I'm making by mixing business and pleasure."

Moira sketched an *X* across her heart. "No, I won't. I promise. I'm taking a break from making judgments. Today I'm just your friend."

It was true. Moira really was the best friend she'd ever had. If it weren't for their professional relationship, Kelly would have spilled everything the second she'd walked into the room.

Finally she sighed. "I didn't believe it was possible, but I am more in love with him than ever."

"In other words, you slept with him," Moira interpreted. "And it was fabulous."

"Beyond fabulous."

"What about Michael? Is he in love with you?"

Kelly wished she could say an unequivocal yes, but the truth was, she'd detected shadows in Michael's eyes this morning. She hadn't pressed for answers, because she honestly hadn't wanted anything to spoil what had been so incredibly magical for her.

"He cares about me," she said slowly. "I know he does."

"And that's enough for you?" her friend asked skeptically.

"It is for now. He still has a lot to sort out. His whole world has changed. He can't go back to doing the work that he loves. He's known that all along, but I think he's just now starting to face the full ramifications. I'm pretty sure he's finally willing to start looking for an alternative line of work, rather than bemoaning what he's lost."

"Facing it could leave him bitter and resentful. He could even blame you—irrationally, I know—for not finding some way to make things turn out differently."

Kelly hadn't even considered that scenario. A man in Michael's position might well look for someone to blame. She frowned at Moira. "Why not blame the sniper who shot him? Why would he ever turn on me?"

"Because the sniper was a faceless enemy. You're right here and you're the person who's supposed to be helping to make him whole again."

"I can only do that within limits," Kelly said defensively.

"I know that, but does he?"

"Of course," Kelly said, but she wasn't entirely certain of it. She set down her half-eaten doughnut and now-cold coffee. Frowning, she added accusingly, "You've certainly managed to put a damper on my good mood."

"I'm sorry. I just want to be sure you're facing facts."

"Possibilities, not facts," Kelly argued.

"You know I only want you to be happy, don't you?" Moira asked, her expression plaintive. "I would never deliberately try to hurt you."

Kelly gave her hand a reassuring squeeze. "I know that, especially since you know I could tell my brother all your secrets," she teased.

"I don't have any secrets," Moira retorted, then grinned. "Darn it all."

Kelly laughed. "I could always make some up."

"I'll think about it. Bryan might respond well to a few hints that my life hasn't been deadly dull up until now. I'd hate for him to get the idea he's saving me from total boredom."

"Sweetie, you travel. You have a successful business. You have friends. I'd hardly call that boring," Kelly chided.

"But your brother has done all sorts of fascinating things," Moira protested.

Kelly shrugged off Bryan's activities. "He's only told you the highlights. Believe me, he spends most of his time with his head buried in these stuffy tomes about dead psychoanalysts or locked away in his office with people who think their lives are a mess."

Moira grinned. "I'm sure he'd love to know how deeply you respect his work."

"I do. He's very good at what he does. It's just not very exciting. He's hardly in a position to cast stones at your life. That's why you're going to be so good for each other. You can spur each other to take some chances, have a few adventures." She winked at her. "Or you can cuddle up together and read all those boring medical and psychology journals side by side in bed, then toss them aside and do far more interesting things."

"Trust me, we have not been sharing the bed with any journals," Moira said, then blushed furiously.

"Told you that you didn't need to worry about being boring," Kelly taunted. "I've got to go. Jennifer's due any second for her therapy and I want a few minutes with her mom first."

Suddenly all business, Moira asked, "How's Jennifer's progress?"

"She's doing great, but her insurance is about to run out. I want to work something out so we can continue with her treatment."

"Let me know if I can help," Moira said. "I'm good at yelling at insurance bureaucrats."

"I may do that." Kelly glanced out the window in the office door and felt her heart skip a beat. Michael was here an hour early and already at work on the parallel bars with no one to spot him. "Gotta run. Michael's out there."

Moira came to stand beside her. "Looks to me as if he's developed a renewed determination to get back on his feet." She gave Kelly a knowing look. "Wonder what—or who—inspired that?"

"I'll let you know if I find out," Kelly said as she walked out and closed the door behind her.

She forced herself to take slow, measured steps across the therapy room, even though she wanted to race over and plant herself in front of Michael to prevent a fall. When she reached him, he'd made his way to the midpoint of the bars. There were white lines of tension around his mouth and furrows of concentration on his brow. She had to resist the urge to yell at him. Instead, she stepped between the bars blocking his path.

"You're ambitious this morning."

A fleeting grin tugged at his lips. "I'm motivated."

"You're overdoing it," she countered.

He regarded her with surprise and a hint of anger. "Don't you think it's about time? I've wasted weeks."

His words cut through her as if they'd been an accusation. "Are you suggesting I haven't worked you hard enough?"

Dismay spread across his face. "No, of course not. I'm the one who's been balking. I haven't gotten with the program, not really. Believe me, I know what tough, rigorous training is like. I can take it and from now on out, I intend to do just that."

Kelly bit back a protest that he might reinjure his leg. She didn't totally understand this sudden need to push himself, but it was obviously important to him. And what were the chances that he might really harm himself?

"I'll make you a deal," she said.

He frowned at that. "Who gave you bargaining rights in this?"

"You did."

"When? When I slept with you?"

She hadn't realized that he had the power to hurt her so badly. Tears stung her eyes, but she blinked them away. "No," she said quietly, "when you hired me as your therapist."

Forgetting about the deal she'd been about to make with him, she whirled around and walked blindly away.

"Kelly!"

She ignored his urgent call, for once glad that he couldn't move quickly enough to stop her. Spotting Jennifer and her mother in the waiting area, she paused long enough to compose herself, plastered a smile on her face and headed their way, certain that Michael wouldn't interrupt. She would have to deal with him again eventually, but by then she could steel herself to do it unemotionally.

And if she couldn't, well, telling him to go to hell would feel really good about now.

Michael knew he'd made a total jackass of himself with Kelly. He wasn't sure why he'd suddenly made the kind of cutting remarks he knew would hurt her. He wished he could blame the entire incident on her thin skin, rather than his own boneheaded behavior, but he couldn't.

Maybe it was the fact that she'd implied he couldn't do the hard work just when his ego was finally convinced it was past time to start pushing his limits. Maybe it was the whole sex thing and the uncomfortable issues it had stirred about the future.

The future. He sighed just thinking about it. He'd put off a visit to the navy doctors for weeks now, despite repeated reminders from the West Coast physicians that he was overdue to check in with the specialists they'd recommended. He couldn't put an examination off forever, even if he didn't want to hear the final, if inevitable, verdict that he'd never go back on active duty.

It was time now. Past time. Sucking it up like the supposedly brave man he was, he made an appointment with the navy doctors he'd been avoiding. He might be dreading it, but he needed an honest assessment of what the future might hold. He wasn't expecting them to tell him anything the doctors in San Diego hadn't said months ago, but he was still holding out hope for a miracle.

The examination was painstakingly thorough, the grim expressions pretty much what he'd expected. He could hang on to his job, as long as he was willing to settle for desk duty.

"I'm sorry," the orthopedic surgeon told him. "I don't see any way around it."

"Not even with intensive physical therapy?" Michael asked, trying to keep a pleading note out of his voice. He'd come here knowing it was time to accept things. He needed to do it and stop fighting for something that could never be.

"Not even then," the man said, removing all hope.

That night, Michael received a call from his commanding officer. "I heard the news," Joe Voinovich told him. "I'm sorry as hell about this."

"Me, too."

"Are you going to take the job they're offering in Washington?"

"No," Michael said flatly. Whatever happened, he was staying in Boston. He'd find something to do eventually. And Kelly was here. Sooner or later he'd coax her to forgive him. Or find the courage to let her go and make some sort of future with a man who had his act together.

The incident at the rehab clinic hadn't been mentioned since it had happened. In the days since, when the time had come for his therapy session, she'd been right on time, a phony smile firmly in place, her voice discernibly chillier than usual. He knew she deserved an apology, but so far he hadn't been able to bring himself to utter one. He was still debating whether it was better to let the relationship die before it really got started.

Then he thought of the way it was between them, the heat and passion, the tenderness and thoughtfulness, and he wasn't sure he could bear it if he lost her. Until he knew what was best, though, the distance between them was safe. In fact, he probably ought to assure that there would be even more distance. He'd let other women go. In fact, he'd made a habit of it. So why was it so difficult to get the words out now?

Maybe because he knew that as soon as he uttered them, he couldn't take them back. He knew they would change everything, that Kelly had enough pride to make her walk away for good, certain that he'd used her and was tossing her aside now that she'd served her purpose.

And wasn't that exactly what he was doing?

"No, dammit." He uttered the words aloud without realizing it.

Kelly's gaze shot toward him. It was one of the rare times lately when she'd looked him in the eye. "What?"

"Nothing," he said. "Talking to myself."

She regarded him with a penetrating look. ''What's wrong?''

Now was the time. He owed her honesty. Hell, he owed her his life.

''There's something we need to talk about,'' he said.

Alarm flashed in her eyes, but she quickly glanced away. When she looked back, there was only mild curiosity in her expression. ''Sure. What?''

He gestured toward a nearby workout bench. ''Let's sit a minute.'' She followed him, her steps dragging ever so slightly. When they were seated, he forced himself to look directly into her eyes. ''I think you know what a lifeline you've been for me,'' he began. ''You've been amazing.''

''But I've outlasted my usefulness,'' she said quietly.

''Don't say it like that,'' he said, hating how the words he'd been struggling to form sounded when she said them with such an air of resignation. She looked as if she might be fighting tears, but she kept her gaze steady.

''But that's the bottom line, isn't it? You want to go on from here on your own.''

''Kelly, you're an incredible woman. You deserve the best and I don't have anything to offer you. I'm getting out of the navy. I have no idea yet what I'll do next. It would be wrong of me to ask you to sit around and wait while I figure things out.''

For a moment, it looked as if she might argue. Michael braced himself to try to counter whatever she said. Instead, though, she sighed, her expression unbearably sad.

"As long as you believe that, then you're right, you don't have anything to offer me."

She stood up, fiddling nervously with the pen she'd been using to make notes on his therapy, not quite looking him in the eye. "Michael, the only thing I ever wanted or needed was your heart."

Chapter Fourteen

Kelly hadn't known it was possible to feel so empty inside. Just when she'd thought she'd finally found something real and permanent and remarkable, Michael had deliberately yanked it away. And why? Because he was so convinced that he was nothing without his stupid uniform, without a job that put his life at risk.

She blamed the Devaneys for having done that to him and she hated them for it. She prayed when Ryan, Sean and Michael eventually found their parents that she would be granted five minutes alone with them to given them a piece of her mind for abandoning those three young boys and destroying their sense of self-worth in the process. It was little wonder that Michael thought he wasn't worthy of being loved by her, when his own parents had drilled that lesson into him at such an early age.

She sighed and turned to find her brother studying her with a worried expression. "What?" she demanded. "Why are you even home tonight? Shouldn't you be with Moira? You've been spending all your free time at her place lately."

Bryan held up his hands. "Hey, don't jump down my throat. I just came over here to ask you if you'd like to come to the pub tonight with Moira and me. Word is you've been holed up here for days now, refusing to go anywhere, including work. Moira's worried sick. Your clients are about to rebel. They don't like any of the substitute therapists she's assigned to them."

Kelly felt a momentary pang of guilt. She knew her clients shouldn't have to suffer because her life was falling apart. "Then I'll go back to work," she said eventually. She could avoid Michael if she only scheduled patients on Mondays, Wednesdays and Fridays at the clinic.

"When?" her brother pressed.

"Soon."

"Whatever that means," he said. "In the meantime, what about tonight? Come with us. You have to start getting out sometime."

She frowned at him. Either he was being deliberately insensitive or he was an awfully lousy psychologist who couldn't even read his own sister.

"Are you crazy?" she asked sourly. "The pub is the very last place I'd ever show my face."

It was his turn to sigh. "I thought so," he said, sinking down in a chair across from her. "Your crummy mood obviously has something to do with Michael. You might as well tell me, Kelly. What did he do to you? I'll kill him."

"Stay out of it," she ordered. "I don't need my big brother fighting my battles for me."

"Then fight them for yourself," he said mildly. "Come with us tonight. Show him that you're not about to let him ruin your life."

"My life is not ruined just because Michael Devaney broke up with me," she said fiercely.

"Then prove it."

"I don't have to prove anything to anybody. I don't want to come to the pub. That's a little too in-your-face for my peace of mind."

"You like it there."

"I liked it there when I was with Michael," she corrected. "If you'd been paying the slightest bit of attention, you'd know that I opted out of spending time there a couple of weeks ago. I didn't want to have to answer a lot of questions when I eventually wound up in exactly the position I'm in now, cast aside by a man who's too self-absorbed or too scared to make a commitment to another living soul. Who needs it?"

"You apparently," Bryan said wryly.

"I don't need Michael," she said emphatically.

"Okay, then, you could meet someone else. There's a guy who's been coming in lately with Maggie's folks. Seems like a good guy." He grinned. "He's almost as handsome as I am."

She frowned at her brother. "That's not saying much."

"Kelly, don't shut yourself away. Michael's my best friend and I love him like a brother, but he's not worth a broken heart."

"Who said anything about my heart being broken?"

He regarded her evenly. "Am I wrong? Tell me I'm wrong and I'll back off. Tell me you have another date tonight, maybe with that doctor you went out with awhile back."

There was no date and she wouldn't lie to him. "Can't you just let me be miserable in peace?"

"Sorry, kid. No can do. Moira and I will pick you up. Be ready at six o'clock."

Her gaze narrowed. "Why so early?"

"It'll be easier if you get there first and stake out your turf. Let Michael be the one who's on the defensive when he finds you there."

What her brother said made a lot of sense, but Kelly wasn't sure she was masochistic enough to take his advice. She'd spend the entire evening being miserable. Why go under those conditions? Why risk having her already aching heart suffer another blow if Michael flat-out ignored her? Staying away would be the smart—safe—thing to do. But she'd never played it safe in her life.

And the pitiful truth was that she desperately wanted to catch a glimpse of Michael, to see if maybe, just maybe, he was as miserable as she was. Maybe by now he'd come to his senses, she thought hopefully, then chastised herself for being an idiot. If Michael had had second thoughts, he knew her phone number and he certainly knew where she lived. He'd started coming there as a teenager.

"I'll go," she told her brother finally, because she found it all but impossible to resist. "But you bring me home the second I ask you to, okay? No questions and no arguments."

"Deal," he said at once. "And if you change your

mind and want me to punch him out, just say the word.''

Kelly sighed. ''Don't even tempt me.''

Michael fully expected a visit from Bryan. In fact, he was looking forward to it. He figured a good thrashing was the least he deserved for hurting Kelly, even if he hadn't meant to, even if he'd thought with some misguided sense of honor that he was protecting her. Instead, though, he heard nothing from his best friend. That left him to sit and stew with his own regrets.

When he finally tired of that, he called his brother. It was time—past time—to act. For a man who'd thrived on action, he'd been way too passive for months now.

''Hey, Ryan, you remember that guy you were telling me about, the one with the charter boats?''

''Sure. You interested after all?'' Ryan asked cautiously.

''Maybe.''

''Want me to set up a meeting?''

Michael drew in a deep breath. It was now or never. Maybe this prospect would turn out to be nothing, but he had to start someplace.

''No,'' he said eventually. ''Is he there tonight?''

''Sure is. You coming by? Everyone's here. We've been missing you. Caitlyn's been asking for you every day.''

Michael felt his mouth curve into the first genuine smile since he'd broken things off with Kelly. ''I can't disappoint my niece, can I? I'll be there in an hour. Have your friend stick around if he can.''

''Will do. See you soon.''

Now that he was committed, he managed to shower and dress in record time. For some reason, his heart felt lighter than it had in months. He should have done something like this long ago, instead of wallowing in self-pity and fear. He was feeling almost upbeat by the time he reached Ryan's Place.

Then he spotted Kelly, sitting at a table separate from the Devaneys and the Havilceks. Bryan and Moira were with her, one on each side as if they felt the need to protect her.

Michael's heart climbed into his throat. She looked fabulous, and sad. Knowing that he was responsible for her sorrow cut right through him. The guilt was almost enough to make him turn tail and run, but he didn't. Tonight was all about getting his act together at long last and Kelly was the reason he couldn't put it off a moment longer.

He forced himself to go right past her table, to stop and utter an impersonal greeting to all three of them, though his gaze never left Kelly's face. Her chin jutted up and she met his gaze without flinching.

"Everything going okay?" he asked her.

"Fine," she said in a terse tone that said everything was far from fine. "I see you're walking with a cane now. That's great progress."

Michael nodded, not sure what to say to that. "I'm here to talk to that friend of Ryan's about a job."

For an instant there was a spark of genuine excitement in her eyes. "The charter boats?"

He nodded.

"I thought you weren't interested in that."

"I've had second thoughts," he told her, his gaze unwavering. "About a lot of things."

"I see," she said, returning to her mask of cool

indifference. "Well, good luck, then." She glanced at Bryan. "I'd like to leave now, if you don't mind."

Bryan cast a hard look at Michael, then stood up. "Sure thing, Kelly. Moira, you want to wait here? I'll be back in ten or fifteen minutes."

Moira nodded. "I'll wait." She gave Michael a pointed look. "Why don't you have a seat?"

"Moira!" Kelly protested sharply, hesitating with her coat halfway on.

"I'm not going to kill him," Moira said. "I can be as civilized as the next person."

Michael grinned at that. "I don't doubt it, but I have a couple of prior engagements, first with my niece and then about a job. You'll have to give me a rain check on the inquisition."

Moira sighed. "Too bad." She stood up and grabbed her coat. "I guess I'll go along with you guys, then."

Michael stood where he was and watched them leave. Kelly never once looked back.

"Woman problems?" Ryan asked sympathetically, coming up beside him.

Michael nodded. "I'm still not sure how I let things get so out of hand. I never meant to hurt her."

"Then fix it," Ryan said simply.

"I'm not sure I know how. I do know that finding a job is the first step, one I have to take for me before I can give any thought at all to the future."

"Does Kelly agree that work should come before her?"

"Probably not," Michael admitted. "But that's the one thing I am sure of."

"Okay, then, let me introduce you to Greg Keith." Ryan led the way across the restaurant to a man seated at a table in the corner. Not until Michael was next to the table did he realize that Greg Keith was in a wheelchair. He had to fight not to show any visible sign of his shock.

Greg grinned at him. "You can ask," he said, when Ryan was gone and Michael had taken a seat opposite him.

"Ask what?"

"About old ironsides here. We've been together a long time now."

"It's none of my business," Michael said.

"It is if you're going to come to work for me. I don't see much point in ignoring my limitations. If I do, then they're controlling me, and believe me, that's not a situation I can tolerate."

Michael nodded. He was just beginning to relate to the sentiment. "What happened?"

"A bullet in the spine during an operation in the Persian Gulf War. I came out of the SEALs with a nice pension and some money in the bank. As soon as I got out of the hospital, I started looking around for a boat to buy. I couldn't imagine my life anywhere except around water. I have a fleet of ten charter boats now, everything from a tall ship to a couple of fishing trawlers." He regarded Michael with a penetrating look. "I assume you're here because Ryan told you I'm always looking for good captains."

Michael nodded slowly, trying to digest what Greg Keith had done with his life once he'd been dealt a devastating blow. It was one more reminder that he had nothing to complain about.

"I'll be honest," he told Greg. "I'm not sure if this is for me, but I'd like to take a look around, see if it feels right."

"Fair enough. Does tomorrow morning suit you?" Greg grinned at Michael. "I guarantee you that once you set foot on deck and get back out to sea, it'll give you a whole new lease on life."

Michael thought of the woman who'd just left the pub and the future that could await them, if he ever found the courage to try. "I truly hope so."

To his shock and ultimately to his relief, Michael discovered that he liked being back on the water, even if he couldn't be heading out to face some sort of incredible danger. The serenity he'd always found at sea hadn't changed just because the type of vessel had.

He also discovered that Greg was a remarkable man, whose accomplishments and whose positive outlook on the hand he'd been dealt quickly became an inspiration to Michael. In no time at all, he felt as if he'd found a new life that was worth living. There was just one thing missing—Kelly.

He finally worked up the nerve to call her, only to be told that she was away on an extended vacation. An hour later, Bryan called him back.

"What the hell were you thinking calling here?" he demanded. "You're the one who made the decision to end things with my sister. Leave her in peace."

"Is she at peace?" Michael dared to ask. If she was, maybe he didn't have any right to try to stir things up again. Maybe the love he felt for her, but hadn't acknowledged in time would never be enough to make things right.

"She's getting there," Bryan said.

"Look, I know I made a lot of mistakes," Michael told him. "I just want a chance to fix things."

"Fix them how?" Bryan asked skeptically.

The truth was that Michael wanted what they'd once had back. He wanted to marry her, but he was not saying that to Bryan before he had a chance to say it to Kelly. Her reaction was the only one that mattered.

"That's between Kelly and me."

"No," Bryan said flatly. "You've done enough to mess up her life. I'm telling you to stay away from her. If our friendship ever meant anything to you, you'll listen to me and do as I ask."

"Sorry, man. You know I respect you, but I don't think I can do that."

"Dammit, Michael, having you walk out on her devastated her. Isn't that enough?"

"I want to make it right," he said again.

"I don't think that's possible," his friend said bluntly. "This vacation she's on, she went with someone."

Michael's heart began to thud dully. "The preppy doctor?"

"I don't think that's any of your business. Just stay away from Kelly, or I'll make you regret it."

Michael might have laughed, if Bryan hadn't sounded so deadly serious. The fact that he was willing to resort to violence to protect his sister told Michael volumes about how badly Kelly had been hurt. Heartsick, he sighed heavily.

"I'll stay away," he promised at last.

Michael kept his promise to Bryan for weeks, going to work seven days a week, hiding out in his apartment during his little bit of free time. He was getting exactly what he deserved for being such a first-class jerk. Kelly had offered him the sun and the moon, to say nothing of her heart, and he'd thrown it all back in her face.

It was a visit from Ryan and Sean that finally pulled him out of his latest bout with self-pity.

"Okay, bro, we've had it," Sean said. "We're tired of waiting for you to come to us, so here we are."

To forestall the pep talk they so clearly intended, Michael offered them beers and some of the large pepperoni pizza that had arrived just ahead of them.

"You're not getting off the hook that easily," Ryan said, as he polished off the last piece of pizza. "We came here, in part at least, because we think it's time to go to Maine and meet Patrick."

The announcement took him by surprise. "Why now?"

"Because of you," Sean said.

"Me? What the hell do I have to do with it?" He looked at Sean. "I thought you wanted to put this meeting off till doomsday, if at all possible."

Sean nodded. "I did till I started seeing how the past is affecting you."

"Nothing in my life has anything whatsoever to do with the past," Michael said emphatically.

"I think you're wrong about that," Ryan said, just as fiercely. "Unless I'm very much mistaken, you've just abandoned a woman you love the same way our parents left us. Maybe it's not even the first time. Don't you think, for your own sake, you need answers so you can break the pattern before you spend the rest of your life alone? I certainly needed a wake-up call to get my life on track. So did Sean. Otherwise, we both might have turned our backs on Maggie and Deanna.''

Michael wasn't interested in their version of pop psychology. ''Are you crazy?'' he demanded. ''Breaking up with Kelly had absolutely nothing to do with the past. If anything, it had to do with the future. It took me a while but I finally got over that. Unfortunately, it was too late.''

''Says who?''

''Her brother.''

Ryan stared at him. ''You took Bryan's word on something that important? What the hell were you thinking?''

''Why would he lie to me?'' Michael asked defensively.

''To protect his sister,'' Sean suggested. ''Geez, bro, that one's so obvious, even I could see it. For an ex-SEAL, you're awfully gullible.''

''He said she went away with someone,'' Michael retorted. ''That sounds as if it's too late to me.''

Sean groaned. ''She did. She and Moira went to Ireland for a week.''

Michael stared. ''Ireland? With Moira?'' He'd given up on her because she'd gone away for a few days with her best friend? Maybe he had been a little too quick to accept the possibility that she didn't care about him because of his past. Maybe he'd bought into the idea that he wasn't worth loving. He could see it so clearly now, how he'd been influenced by his parents' abandonment. After all, if they had found him so unlovable, then sooner or later wouldn't Kelly likely reach the same conclusion? Why fight for someone he was destined to lose anyway? If that had been his thinking when he took Bryan's words at face value, then he really was pitiful.

As for Bryan's role in all this by deliberately misleading him, Michael resolved to deal with that later.

He stood up suddenly and headed for the door. "You guys stick around and finish your beers," he told his brothers. "I've got someplace I need to be."

"Think he's going out for more pizza?" Sean joked.

"Not if he's half as smart as I think he is," Ryan retorted.

Michael grinned at them. "I'm smart enough to go after the best thing that ever happened to me."

"Of course you are," Ryan confirmed. "Whatever the past, at least the three of us have started a new Devaney family tradition."

"What's that?" Michael asked.

"We hang on to the people we love."

Chapter Fifteen

The trip to Ireland had been everything Kelly had always imagined it would be, but she hadn't enjoyed herself. An image of a dark-haired, moody Irishman back home kept intruding. If it hadn't been for Moira, she would have cut the trip short and gone home early.

But to what? she wondered despondently. She had her work, of course, but there would be no social life, not as long as the memory of one man refused to let her alone. She'd never been the type who could counter a broken heart with a whirlwind of dating, especially when none of the men ever measured up. Maybe she needed to accept the fact that she was a one-man woman and always had been.

She looked across the table in the pub where she and Moira were having dinner and saw that her best friend was regarding her with a worried frown, the same frown she'd been wearing for most of the trip.

"We might as well go home," Moira said with resignation. "You're obviously having a terrible time."

"Don't be silly," Kelly said, instantly consumed with guilt. "I'm not going to spoil your vacation by cutting it short."

"Believe me, that would probably be better than traveling from village to village with a woman who's not really seeing the scenery."

"I'm sorry."

"Don't be sorry. Suggesting this trip was probably a bad idea in the first place. I just wanted to get you away from all the bad memories in Boston for a while. Bryan agreed it was a good idea."

"Bryan was just scared I'd cave in and go looking for Michael," Kelly said.

"Would you have done that?"

Kelly sighed heavily. "More than likely. I love him. I can't help it. I think I've loved him since I was a kid. These past few months have only deepened what I feel for him."

"The man hurt you," Moira reminded her, sounding as fiercely protective as Bryan would.

"I know," Kelly acknowledged. "But he didn't do it intentionally. I all but threw myself at him before he was ready to think about anything but getting back on his feet again. I was ready for a relationship. He wasn't."

"And you think that's changed by now?"

"I honestly don't know, but there's only one way to find out."

This time it was Moira who sighed deeply. "By

going home," she concluded. "We can make the arrangements to leave in the morning."

Kelly knew her friend would do that, too, but she couldn't let her. "I have a better idea. Let's call Bryan and see if he can't come over here and join you. I know the two of you were planning a trip together before you decided to rescue me. When he gets here, then I'll leave. Until then, I'll try to throw myself into the spirit of things." She glanced toward the small dance floor. "I might even try an Irish jig."

There was no mistaking the faint spark of excitement that stirred in Moira's eyes. "I can live without watching you trip over your own feet," she said wryly. "As for calling Bryan, are you sure you wouldn't mind going back alone?"

"I'm a big girl. I can fly by myself," Kelly responded with a chuckle. "Stop worrying. I'm not going to throw open the door and dive into the Atlantic."

Moira regarded her indignantly. "Well, I should certainly hope not."

"A couple of weeks ago, I wouldn't have been so quick to say that," Kelly said. "But now I'm going to go home and fight for the man I love. He's not going to know what hit him."

Moira finally grinned. "Good for you."

"It might be best, though, if we don't tell Bryan that," Kelly warned her. "It might give him second thoughts about coming over here to join you."

A blush tinted Moira's cheeks. "Oh, I think I can keep your brother's mind otherwise occupied."

Kelly studied her friend and noted the new sense of confidence. It made her more attractive than ever.

"Yes, I imagine you can. Any hint of wedding bells?"

"Not yet," Moira conceded. "But then I haven't taken him on my tour of quaint Irish chapels yet. That ought to get him thinking along the right lines."

"Maybe you'd be better off just asking him outright to marry you," Kelly suggested. "Bryan's head is usually in the clouds. The direct approach has its advantages with a man like that."

"Is that what you intend to do with Michael, ask him to marry you?"

"Absolutely not," Kelly said as if she were utterly horrified by the idea. Then she grinned. "Actually I intend to plant the idea in his head and then let him think he was the one who came up with it. Michael has definite control issues, but now's not the time to work on them."

Moira lifted her glass of ale. "To us, then, and the men we love."

"To love," Kelly said, then added silently, and to getting Michael to believe in it.

Well, this was turning out to be damned frustrating, Michael decided as he spent days trying to catch up with Kelly.

He'd finally heard she was back from Ireland… from his mother. Apparently Kelly had paid her a visit on her return. She'd brought Doris Havilcek a lovely book of Irish recipes.

And Kelly had been spotted at the pub. Maggie reported that Kelly had dropped by with a list of Irish musicians who had upcoming tours to the United States and would be happy to play at Ryan's Place.

There had been sightings at the clinic, as well. Jennifer told him shyly that Kelly had been there for her last session, which had been rescheduled from Tuesday to Wednesday, a day when he wasn't likely to be around.

His plan for getting to Kelly and making things right was being foiled at every turn. He was mentally threatening to stake out her parents' place, when he concluded that maybe he needed to put a little more thought into his approach. It certainly wouldn't hurt to have a specific plan in mind.

Years of SEAL training had taught him that every last detail of an operation had to be ironed out in advance to assure success, even if the best-laid plans occasionally went wildly awry and he wound up scrambling. Looking at the alternatives from every angle might mean delaying the start of the mission, but it could guarantee achieving the results he wanted.

While he was at home pondering the best way to handle things, he got a call from an admiral at the Pentagon requesting a meeting.

"Sir, I've already resigned," he pointed out.

"I've got the paperwork right here on my desk," Admiral Stokes agreed. "Haven't signed it yet."

Michael bit back a curse at the delay. He'd wanted the ties severed once and for all. "Why is that, sir?"

"It occurs to me that you might not be thinking too clearly after what you've been through."

"Believe me, I've been over this a thousand times," Michael countered. "I'm not suited to a desk job. Whatever contribution I was able to make to the navy came because I was a highly skilled operative. That's over."

"Hell, man, your brain still functions, doesn't it?"

The harsh tone cut right through Michael and made him sweat. "Yes, of course, but—"

"Oh, stop trying to make excuses and get down to D.C.," Stokes commanded. "We've spent too much damned time and money training you to think like a SEAL to have you wasting it by running a bunch of tourists around so they can catch some fish."

Michael didn't waste time asking how the admiral knew what he'd been up to.

"We need to talk," Stokes continued. "Be here at oh-eight-hundred hours. And that's an order, Lieutenant. You're not out of the navy yet."

"Yes, sir," Michael said and slowly hung up the phone. To his astonishment, rather than fury over the presumptive arrogance of the admiral, what he felt was a faint stirring of excitement.

Kelly was feeling really pleased with herself. She'd made very sure that Michael knew she was back in town, while managing to avoid him catching so much as a glimpse of her. If she knew him half as well as she thought she did, he was probably going a little crazy by now. The fact that he'd been trying to catch up with her added to her conviction.

She had one last stop she wanted to make, possibly the riskiest one of all, because she wasn't entirely sure she could avoid getting caught this time. She headed to Greg Keith's charter boat headquarters, ostensibly to make an inquiry about chartering a boat that was captained by Michael. She wanted him to hear about the request, wanted him to wonder why she'd suddenly decided to take up fishing.

"To be honest," Greg told her, "I'm not so sure

Mr. Devaney's going to be taking out any more fishing charters.''

Kelly stared at him in shock. The announcement was the last thing she'd expected when she'd come here. "He's not? Why? Did something happen? He's not injured again, is he? His recovery is still on track?"

The ex-SEAL, whom Ryan had willingly sent her to, grinned at the barrage of questions. The smile transformed his face from a rugged ruin to something intriguingly handsome.

"Whoa," he ordered. "Don't panic. Michael's fine. It's just that he's gone out of town for a few days, and I'm not sure what's going to come of the trip."

"He went away on business? What kind of business?" The only kind of business Michael had, as far as she knew, was SEAL business.

"I'm not at liberty to discuss it. Why not ask him yourself when he gets back?"

"When will that be?"

"Hard to say," he said with a shrug. He seemed to be enjoying her growing agitation. "Should I tell him you've been by asking a lot of questions? Men usually like to know when a beautiful woman's been poking around in their life."

Kelly slapped a business card on his desk. "Yes, indeed, you be sure to tell Michael that I came by. And tell him that I am interested in chartering a boat, but only if he's at the helm."

"Got it," Greg said, his grin spreading.

She was at the door, when he called after her. She turned around and saw him studying her card.

"If things don't work out between you and Michael," he said, "you give me a call. Something tells me you're the kind of woman who only comes around once in a man's lifetime.''

She laughed. ''Tell that to Michael. See what he says.''

His dark, serious gaze never wavered. ''I just might do that.''

Oh, my, Kelly thought. Greg Keith might be confined to a wheelchair, but he could definitely give a woman a run for her money. If he reported their encounter to Michael the way she intended, she'd have to reciprocate by finding him a woman who'd be up to the challenge.

Michael was still in a daze when he got back from Washington. The admiral had been extraordinarily persuasive. Michael had left his office with a promotion to lieutenant commander and a job in the counterterrorism intelligence unit, working out of Boston. Being able to stay close to his family had sealed the deal. His days of fishing were pretty much over. He'd enjoyed the work, but he couldn't honestly say he regretted the dramatic turn things had taken during his Pentagon visit.

Now he just had to get Kelly on board. En route to her place, he took three detours: one to a jeweler's, one to a florist's and one to Greg's office to resign.

Greg took one look at the bouquet and grinned. ''For me? You shouldn't have.''

''Very funny.''

''I don't suppose those are for Kelly Andrews, are they?''

Michael froze in place. ''What do you know about Kelly?''

''She stopped by while you were gone. She wanted

to charter a fishing boat for the day, with you as captain.''

''Are you serious?'' he asked incredulously.

''I am. She seemed to be, too. Attractive woman. You going after her?''

Michael nodded. He was definitely going after her, though before he proposed, he might ask what the hell she thought she'd been up to the past couple of weeks. If he didn't know for a fact that she believed in the direct approach, he might have concluded she'd been deliberately taunting him.

Greg gave him a penetrating look. ''I assume I can cross you off my list of available captains, then?''

''In more ways than one,'' Michael said. ''I really appreciate you giving me a job, Greg. It helped to get my confidence back in ways I can't even begin to explain.''

''You staying in the navy?''

Michael nodded. ''I'm just discovering that there's more than one way to skin an enemy. You ought to think about that.''

''Not me. I like my laid-back lifestyle. You go on and get the bad guys.'' He winked. ''And while you're at it, good luck with getting the girl.''

''Thanks, pal. I'll be by from time to time and I'm sure I'll see you at the pub.''

''Count on it.''

From the office, Michael headed for home to change, then went straight to Kelly's. When he finally showed up at her door, he was in his dress uniform and carrying a bouquet of spring flowers that had cost an arm and a leg in midwinter.

When she opened the door, there was a brief moment when he thought she might turn right around and slam it in his face. Instead, she squared her shoulders and stood fast. That little display of courage made him want to scoop her up and kiss her, but he resisted the urge.

"Can I help you?" she asked.

She spoke in a cool tone that didn't quite go along with her recent forays into all the corners of his life. Still, it was disconcerting. Suddenly hesitant, he thrust the flowers toward her and said, "I brought you these."

She accepted them with apparent reluctance, breathed in the sweet scent, then looked at him over the extravagant bouquet. "Why?"

He shifted uneasily at her lack of enthusiasm. "Could we go inside?" He didn't want a lot of witnesses if she turned him down flat.

She shook her head. "I don't think so. I see you're wearing your uniform. Does that mean you're going back to work for the navy?"

He nodded. "I'll tell you about that in a minute. The important thing is, I'm gainfully employed again."

"I thought you were gainfully employed by Greg Keith."

His lips twitched. "Yeah, I heard you'd paid him a visit. What's with the sudden desire to go fishing?"

"I'm exploring new interests. I thought it might be fun."

"And spending the day at sea with me had nothing to do with it?"

"Not really."

"Then why didn't you go through with the charter?"

She shrugged. "Changed my mind."

"That's not the way I hear it, Kelly."

"Men have a tendency to imagine things and then exaggerate," she told him.

"I see. Okay, then, let's get back to the reason I'm here."

"I figured you wanted me to know you'd gone back to work for the navy," she said. "Now I know. Did you really think that mattered to me?"

"No, but settling into a career mattered to me," he said.

"And fishing's not good enough?"

"No, dammit. Stop twisting everything I say. It wasn't about money, Kelly. Or about prestige. It was about self-respect. I need to do something that matters."

A flicker of understanding warmed her eyes, but then that shuttered expression fell back into place. "I'm happy for you, truly I am, but if that's all you came to tell me, I need to get going."

She was about to close the door, when Michael jammed his foot in it. "Wait."

She looked into his eyes.

"I love you," he said, blurting it out before he messed up again. "*That's* what I came to tell you. That and to ask you to marry me." He fumbled in his pocket and drew out a ring, a diamond solitaire that could never in a million years match the sparkle in her eyes when she was happy. "I know I'm the worst sort of fool and I don't deserve you, but no one will ever love you more or work harder to make you happy."

Her eyes unexpectedly filled with tears and made his heart wrench.

"Are you sure, Michael?" she asked, her voice

shaky. "Really, really sure? Because this is it. If you take it back this time, I will never forgive you."

"I won't take it back," he promised, hardly daring to believe that he'd finally gotten it right. "I love you and I want to marry you." He searched her face, looking for a clue about what she was feeling. "If you'll have me. Will you, Kelly?"

She stepped toward him then and lifted her hand to his cheek. "Oh, Michael," she whispered, "all you ever had to do was ask."

Epilogue

"I still don't understand why you're in such a hurry," Bryan said to Michael as he ran a finger around the collar of his tuxedo. "I know my sister. If she hasn't changed her mind about you after all these years, she's not going to. There's no rush."

Michael frowned at him. He'd had enough trouble waiting the month Kelly had insisted it would take her to plan the perfect wedding. "I take it you're in no big hurry to get Moira to the altar."

Bryan stared at him blankly. "Married? Me and Moira?"

"You haven't even considered it? I thought you were in love with her."

"I am, at least I think I am. I'm not even sure I know what love is."

"And you're a psychologist," Michael said, shaking his head. "I pity your clients."

"Wait a minute, how did we go from discussing this rush into marriage you and Kelly are taking to picking apart my relationship with Moira?"

"Just a diversionary tactic," Michael admitted cheerfully. "Plus, if you were in love, you'd understand why we don't want to wait. Too bad, because I really thought you and Moira had something special. Mind if I introduce her to someone at the reception?"

Bryan's expression turned dark. "Forget about it."

Michael gave his best man a triumphant look. "*That,* my friend, is love."

Bryan looked vaguely bemused by his analysis. "Do you suppose that's why she kept dragging me into all those little churches all over Ireland? Was she trying to tell me something?"

"I'd say that's a safe bet," Michael said, regarding him with a pitying look. "Have a couple of glasses of champagne at the reception and ask her."

"Ask her what?"

"Ask her to marry you, idiot."

"Oh." A slow smile spread across Bryan's face. "Maybe I will at that."

Kelly stood at the back of the church and studied the man waiting for her in front of the altar, his back ramrod straight, his cane nowhere in sight. He was stunning in his uniform, but he was darned good-looking out of it, too. In fact, she preferred him that way, naked and eager. A blush climbed into her cheeks at the wicked thought. On her wedding day and in church, no less. She was surprised a bolt of lightning didn't strike her dead on the spot. Then, again, she was about to marry the man. Why do that, if he didn't get to her?

"You ready, pumpkin?" her father asked.

"Absolutely," she said without hesitation.

"Have been for a long time, haven't you? Michael's always been the one."

"Always," she agreed. "This just proves teenage fantasies can come true."

"Not without a little nudge from your brother," he reminded her. "You given him the credit he's due?"

She feigned a frown. "I gave him my best friend and he's too dense to make the most of it. Do you know Moira came back from Ireland without a ring on her finger?"

"Stop fretting about that," Moira said when she overheard Kelly's complaint. "It's your wedding day. Enjoy it. I know I intend to. I've already spotted three gorgeous men who came without dates."

Kelly grinned. "You go, girl."

Her father shook his head. "If I'm not mistaken, it's time for all of us to go. Isn't that the wedding march starting up now?" He leaned down and pressed a kiss to Kelly's cheek. "Be happy, pumpkin."

"I will be," she said with absolute confidence. She looked at Michael and caught his eye. His gaze was filled with so much love, it made her knees weak.

The Havilceks must have spotted it, too, because Doris Havilcek smiled, tears in her eyes, and even her husband looked as if he might shed a tear or two when Michael took several steady steps to meet her partway down the aisle and take her arm.

Behind them were the Devaneys—Ryan, Maggie and Caitlyn next to Sean, Deanna and Kevin. There was a third dark-haired man there, as well, a man who was unmistakably from the same gene pool. Kelly shot a curious glance toward Michael.

"Patrick?" she mouthed.

Michael nodded. "I didn't want to say anything, because I wasn't sure he would come. We went up to Maine and all but dragged him down here. We told him this was a family occasion, and that the Devaneys stick together now."

"Are you happy he's here?"

"I'm reserving judgment. Patrick has some issues. I don't want them affecting the rest of us. And before you ask, I am not getting into that right here when the priest is about to marry us."

Kelly grinned. "Oh, right. I almost forgot."

"As if," he said dryly. "You've been planning this day since the day you ignored my temper tantrum and walked into my apartment."

"Longer, actually," she confessed unrepentantly. "I love you, Michael Devaney."

Kelly repeated those words during the ceremony, then added, "And I will make your family mine—the Havilceks, and each and every one of your brothers and their families." She cast a look toward Patrick, who managed to appear removed from all the others even though only inches separated him on the pew from Ryan. "We're stronger together than we are apart."

"Amen," Michael said softly.

The priest beamed at them. "Then I now pronounce you man and wife. May you live in love all the days of your lives."

"No question about it," Michael whispered just before he kissed her until her toes curled.

"No question at all," Kelly agreed.

There were discoveries to be made and challenges to be met. The future stretched out before them with all its bumps and twists and turns, but their love would remain constant. She was sure of that. Gazing deep into Michael's blue eyes, she saw that he finally believed it, too.

*   *   *   *   *

Don't miss Patrick Devaney's story,
PATRICK'S DESTINY,
in the fourth book of Sherryl Woods's
exciting new miniseries,
THE DEVANEYS,
which features five brothers torn apart in
childhood, reunited by love.

On sale July 2003 from
Silhouette Special Edition.

Chapter One

Alice had never been so humiliated and embarrassed in her life. Not only had she lost control of her students and let one of them nearly drown, she had done it in front of Patrick Devaney.

Everyone in Widow's Cove knew that Patrick had turned into a virtual recluse. He lived on that fishing boat of his, ate his meals at Jess's, and, for all Alice knew, drank himself into oblivion there every night, as well. What no one knew was why.

She almost hadn't recognized him when he'd emerged from the ocean dripping wet and mad as the dickens. His hair was too long and stubble shadowed his cheeks. He looked just a little disreputable and more than a little dangerous, especially with his intense blue eyes shooting angry sparks.

Alice remembered a very different Patrick from high school. Even though she'd been two years older, everyone at the county high school knew each other at least by sight. Even as a sophomore, Patrick had been the flirtatious, wildly popular star football player; his brother Daniel, the captain of the team. The two of them had been inseparable. Now they barely spoke. No one understood that, either.

Oddly enough, though, even when he'd been lambasting her for what had happened this afternoon, Alice had felt a strange sort of kinship with Patrick. And despite his insistence that he was as much at fault for the incident as she was, she knew he'd merely been letting her off the hook.

That was why the second that school was out for the day she went back to her house, filled a container with some of the beef vegetable soup she'd made the night before and a loaf of her home-baked bread and headed right back to Patrick Devaney's private, no-trespassing dock. She took a certain perverse pleasure in pushing open the flimsy gate and making a lot of noise as she approached his trawler. She wasn't the least bit surprised when he emerged from below deck with a scowl firmly in place.

"Which part of stay away didn't you understand?" he inquired, blocking her way.

"I figured it didn't apply to me, since I come bearing gifts," she said cheerfully, holding out the soup and bread. "You never mentioned the fact that you were in that freezing ocean because of me—"

"Because of Ricky," he corrected.

She shrugged at the distinction. "I thought some hot soup might ward off a chill. I don't want it on my conscience if you get sick because of what happened."

His mouth curved into an arrogant grin that made her heart do an unexpected flip.

"I don't get sick," he informed her.

"Good for you," she replied. "Having some nutritious soup won't hurt."

"You casting aspersions on Molly's chowder?"

"Hardly, but you must be tired of that by now."

The grin faded. "Meaning?"

She faltered. She hadn't meant to admit that she knew anything about his habits. "She says you're there a lot, that's all."

"You asked about me?" he asked, not even attempting to hide his surprise. The arrogant tilt to his mouth returned.

"I most certainly did not. Molly tends to volunteer information she thinks will prove helpful."

He sighed. "Yeah. I keep talking to her about that. She seems to think she can save me from myself if she gets enough people pestering me."

"What do you think?" Alice asked curiously.

"That I don't need saving."

She laughed. "I keep telling her the same thing. It hasn't stopped her yet."

"No, and I imagine she'll want to know exactly how polite I was when you came over here, and I'll hear about it if I send you away." He pushed off from the railing and held out his hand. "You want to come aboard and share a bowl of that soup? Looks to me like there's plenty for two."

Alice hesitated, then reached out to accept his outstretched hand as she stepped on board. She noted that the boat was spotless. Every piece of chrome and wood had been polished to a soft sheen. Fishing nets were piled neatly. Apparently Patrick Devaney used the time he didn't spend socializing or shaving to pay close attention to his surroundings.

Below deck in the small cabin, it was the same. The table was clear except for the half-filled coffee cup from which he'd apparently been drinking. The bed a few feet away was neatly made, the sheets crisp and clean, a navy-blue blanket folded precisely at the foot of the bed.

Moving past her in the tight space, Patrick took a pot from a cupboard, poured the soup into it and set it on the small two-burner stove, then retrieved two bowls and spoons from the same cupboard. Alice was all too aware of the way he filled the cramped quarters, of the width of his shoulders, of the narrowness of his hips. It was the first time in ages she'd recognized the powerful effect pure masculinity could have on her.

From the moment she'd lost her parents on the same awful night nearly a year ago, she'd gone into an emotional limbo. She let no one or nothing touch her. She even kept a barrier up between herself and her students, or at least she had until Ricky Foster had scared the living daylights out of her this afternoon. Nothing had rattled her so badly since the night the police had called to tell her that her parents were dead.

Don't go there, she thought, forcing her attention back to the present. One appreciative, surreptitious glance at Patrick's backside as he bent to retrieve something from the tiny refrigerator did the trick. It was all she could do not to sigh audibly at the sight.

Don't go there, either, she told herself very firmly. She was here for penance and for soup. Nothing more. A peek at Patrick Devaney sent another little shock of awareness through her and proved otherwise.

Oh, well, there was certainly no harm in looking, she decided as she sat back and enjoyed the view. Even a woman in a self-imposed state of celibacy had the right to her fantasies.

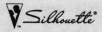

SPECIAL EDITION™

Continues the captivating series
from *USA TODAY* bestselling author

SUSAN MALLERY

**These heart-stoppin' hunks are rugged,
ready and able to steal your heart!**

Don't miss the next irresistible books in the series...

COMPLETELY SMITTEN
On sale February 2003
(SE #1520)

ONE IN A MILLION
On sale June 2003
(SE #1543)

Available at your favorite retail outlet.

Where love comes alive™

If you enjoyed what you just read,
then we've got an offer you can't resist!

Take 2 bestselling love stories FREE!

Plus get a FREE surprise gift!

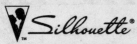

COMING NEXT MONTH